MW00935040

About the Author

Once, while working part-time as a cashier at a craft store, Lee Bradford was handed a purple bag by an elderly woman purchasing scrapbooking materials. The bag contained fresh dog droppings. This, readers, was a lesson in foreshadowing.

GOOD CLEAN DIRT

Good, Clean Dirt

by Lee Bradford
Copyright © Lee Bradford
 and Cannibal Coalition

Cover design by Lee Bradford

All characters and events in this
publication are fictitous. Any re-
semblance to real persons, living
or dead, is purely coincidental

The names have been changed to protect the injuriously maladaptive.

His parents had expectations of him when they named him 'Reuben'- a name that evoked, to them, images of grand, dynamic paintings and large women. He was going to do great things, inspire people, make history. They were going to be so proud of him.

The lesson that Reuben took away from it, however, was that he went well with rye. Serendipity would have it that, when he was older, there was a bar across the street from his 'Cash for Gold' outfit and it was a rare day that he was not found with a gin and tonic after closing hours. But to say that drunkenness was his greatest flaw would be an insult to his other flaws, which he treated equally.

It was alright to have a drink every night, he justified. It's not like he was using his own money.

He was just the right amount of crooked to be ranked beneath underlings in the hierarchy of organized crime. His place in the chain of command meant that he never had to talk to Moretti and never had to deal with the consequences of being tied to the boss. The entire relationship benefitted him, for all he was concerned, and his work was simple.

Every once in awhile, a package would appear on his doorstep with no return address. It would be full of money. Reuben wasn't a fool- he knew a raised bill when he saw one. And with the string of bank heists in the past few years it wasn't that hard to figure out what was happening. Any idiot could bleach a ten and reprint it as a twenty: no one checks to see which president is actually in the corner pocket.

He found the idea that they were stealing physical dollars to be a charming touch of antiquity when identity theft was so much easier. That's how he know he had a boss with convictions. At least seven of them in the state of Pennsylvania, but no one was going to say that out loud where someone could hear it.

It was easy to have a high payout when your money was funny. This was the agreement- he gets the reputation of the highest payout on his side of town in exchange for legitimate goods, takes them to a real dealer that pays real money, and he gets to keep 40%. The only time he ever had to see anyone about anything was when they came to pick up the profits, and they always came in looking like customers.

To any onlooker, he seemed unaffiliated. It was only Reuben who knew their faces.

The sorts of people who know the power of money come in two types: those who sit in comfy office chairs overlooking the vast city sprawl from an office building that serves no purpose other than to make more money for the man sitting in the comfy chair, and those who meet in back rooms or darkened alleys under code names like Needles and The Shark.

It was entirely possible that Needles got his name from a drug history, and it was even more probable that he got it from his likeness. He was thin, with a long face and a long nose and long fingers- all of which made him look like an urban legend instead of a living, breathing person with very bad teeth. Finding clothes that fit must have been a nightmare, and he often settled for jeans and a tee shirt underneath an ill-fitting suit-jacket.

The Shark looked more like a bear than anything, but 'Sam the Bear' didn't alliterate and was already taken by a local radio personality. But it made sense to those that named him, if no one else, because Sam hailed from Hawai'i and the majority of people held a vast misunderstanding of how dangerous sharks really were. Sharks, being rather harmless when you leave them alone, were a horrible choice. Sam, on the other hand, was dangerous at any given moment.

Which brings us to Reuben, who thought he was named after a sandwich and looked like he'd been dressed in a hurry by the late 90's and then overcome with a massive hangover. He, himself, was suffering from a hangover this morning. Now that it has been mentioned, it was also a rare sight to see Reuben in a manner that did not seethe the phrase 'regret' in one manner or another.

But instead of meeting in a dark alley, they were taking up space in the back room of Reuben's shop- a room designated for two things: counting the money and meeting with Needles and the Shark. Well, three things if you counted the cot in the corner.

"Alright," Needles began, with the Shark standing behind him just in case. In case of what, really, was kind of a stretch when it is considered that Reuben was neither tall nor strong and often gave off the impression of being a distant cousin to the rodent family. "You're probably wondering what the sitiation is."

It was rare that they would ever contact him outside of their passive exchanges. If there was a Meeting, of any sort, then that meant that it was not about money laundering. It meant that he had a Job To Do.

9

So when Needles dropped a handful of photographs down on the white folding table, Reuben was certain that someone had made The Boss a touch touchier than usual.

The photographs were of a mean-looking guy, standing taller than even The Shark: very tall, very square. Reuben peered over his sunglasses at the photos, thinking that maybe it would cut the glare from the lights in his office. No, the photos were just awful, blurry pieces of shit taken from behind bushes and around corners. Most of the shots got just enough detail to tell that the subject of the photo had dreadlocks reaching to the middle of his back.

"So who is he," Reuben asked.

"This is Lou Rhodes. And he used to be one of Mr Moretti's hired muscle." Needles was on a last-name basis with The Boss. Reuben knew his name, he just never saw any point in saying it. He peered at the fuzzy photos on the table. Yeah, he could see it. Sort of: he at least looked like all of the other big, muscle-lumbering men that he'd seen accompany anyone associated with Moretti. "But he dropped off the face of the earth awhile back and they think he might be talkin' to some cops."

Reuben frowned, still trying to shake the last bit of drunkenness from his head. "Please don't say you want me to kill him," he said. You don't ask money launderers to kill people unless you're really scraping the bottom of the barrel.

Needles smiled, showing him every single one of his rotting teeth. "Don't worry yourself, Weller. We know that you're not an assassin." Reuben held his breath, waiting for the other shoe to drop. "We want you to spy on him. We gotta know two things- is he doing business with someone else and is he talking to the cops. Someone got us tangled up in some foreign arms dealing and we think he might be the guy. The Boss doesn't think he's a threat. We need to make sure."

"You got me spying on this guy?" Needles nodded. "How dangerous is he?"

Needles was sucking on his teeth a little. "He's only dangerous if you piss him off, so you'll be able to get close if you need to. Just don't let him know what you're doing."

Well, that much was a given. "What's the payout?"

"You'd have to close your shop for a few days if you want to catch him. We'd be happy to reimburse the potential payout and an additional one-hundred dollars per day for… inconvenience."

Reuben swished the idea around in his mouth. He could do better. "Make it two-hundred. Having to abandon my store this close to the end of the month when people's rent is due is mighty inconvenient."

Needles didn't seem to like this game very much, but after some thought, he nodded. "We can do two hundred," he said.

"And my payout per day runs about ten grand." He gave them a sideways grin. Needles groaned.

"This is the address that he was last seen at," Needles said, handing him a slip of paper.

Reuben reached for it carefully, as if one false move might stick him with one of his fingers and infect him with whatever was afflicting his teeth. Needles pulled it back just before he could take it, causing him to tumble forward. "These better be some damn good shots," he warned.

"You asked me to do them," Reuben said,

11

snatching the address from his fingers. The Shark took a step forward and Reuben sank back into his chair before he risked getting his lungs ripped right out. (There had been a rumor, of course, but no one could confirm nor deny whether Sam The Shark kept the lungs of someone who looked at him funny once. But it was always a good idea to be on the safe side, especially when he weighs the bulk of three of you.)

"Well, I believe that's all," Needles said. "Can't get those photos if we're holdin' you here, now can we?" He stood, The Shark followed, and they left Reuben Weller alone in his office. He sat back in his chair, putting his feet up on the table and running a few numbers in his head. Ten grand a day plus two-hundred for 'inconvenience.' The trick was… how long could he keep up the charade that he was actually working and not just sitting around while the cash piled up.

The first day was going to be dedicated to traveling to this… sad little mountain town he was holing up in. And it wasn't going to be hard to get a better shot of him than whoever had decided that a brown blur was enough to go by in the first photos. He'd be done in hours with some creative staging.

He leaned back and smiled. And to think that there were people out there that had to work for a living. What chumps.

What absolute chumps.

At Least Four Cat-owners Have Bought That Damn Figurine.

Reuben had never heard of Harrenville, and it was no wonder: it was barely a dot on the map, taking up approximately two square miles in the mountains and it looked to be mostly dead trees. To get there, he had to drive through a series of switchbacks with no railing. His station wagon was not built to accommodate sharp turns and he was thankful that he was, for one, going uphill and not down and for two, the only person on this road.

He was solidified in the fact that the only people who would ever be on this god-forsaken road was if they were looking to kill themselves or if they were never intending on leaving. Even if he didn't do any actual climbing, Reuben was exhausted by the time he got to the top.

The incline flattened to something a little more forgiving on his hydraulics. The road was elevated a good twenty feet above the actual soil. He whizzed over the top of a massive white building, easily identified as a factory of some kind- although it was unclear what exactly a place named Syracor might do. The black and bare earth even made the white walls of it seem dirty, even moreso with the bright lights shining straight onto it. He didn't really see the point in the twenty-foot fence, nor the barbed wire coiled around the top of it

13

like a vine. Who would want to break into a factory?

Harrenville was nestled in a small valley between ridges, giving the impression that the lights from
houses might actually be stars being held there by the
mouth of the mountain. It was only 9:00, but there
didn't seem to be many lights on, even in the middle of
the summer. Small towns turn in early, he guessed.

Driving down the street in downtown was just
so… sad in comparison to driving around in the city.
There was no one on the streets, either. The only things
that he spotted that were open this late seemed to be gas
stations and hotels.

Well, he wasn't about to stay at a hotel. That
was a perfectly good way to waste most of his compen-
sation money. The back seat of his station wagon was
just as good as a bed in his definition.

Instead, he found Rosemary Lane, where Lou
was last seen, and parked at the Sav-A-Lot across the
street. Road-weary, he climbed into the back seat with
a bottle of vodka and fell asleep to the quietest night he
had ever experienced.

See, he could tell that this was a really nice part
of town because when he woke up there was a pamphlet
advertising a homeless shelter. He woke to two of them
flapping in the wind from his view between the gap
in the front seats. One had Jesus on the back of it. He
stared at Jesus waving at him from his cross for a good
thirty minutes before Reuben had settled that he wasn't
intent on waving back. He lifted his head, almost immediately wanting to put it back down again, and slowly
remembered why he was sleeping in the back of his car
this time.

Oh right- money.

And the nearly-empty town that he'd rode into the night before was now crawling with people. Hundreds of them of all ages just milling about in the street like they didn't mind blocking traffic. However, the traffic seemed to be curiously missing. He squinted in the late morning sun.

The entire street seemed to be blocked off for some kind of… event- the kind with lots of tents and the smell of grilling meat. About twenty feet from his car was a white tent that seemed to be selling home-made dog biscuits and cat toys. It made the place smell musty. The stall next to them was selling jam.

The concept of a Farmer's Market wasn't completely lost on him- he knew what they were in theory. Honestly, he liked the idea of selling shit at a 100% markup- he just wasn't very good at coming up with a product that anyone would want. If he knew a thing or two about farming he might just sell vegetables, but he didn't know the first thing about farming, let alone the second.

He'd just never been to one before. He'd never thought that people would actually line up for home-made salsa mixes. And everyone was so… friendly. The stall owners were chatting up customers instead of rushing them out the door. People seemed… genuinely happy to live in this town.

What a weird place this was. Reuben didn't think he could handle that kind of life: everyone knowing everyone, going to the market on Saturday, turning in at 9pm because that was when they rolled up the sidewalks. He'd turn out to be the black sheep before he even unpacked.

He thought the present lack of vegetables kind of odd. It was the middle of summer. Didn't vegetables come from summer?

But that wasn't important. What was important was finding this Lou guy and getting some good dirt on him.

He was pretty sure no one actually lived downtown, but with his car blocked in from the market there wasn't much of a way to go looking for Lou unless he wanted to explore the entire town on his own. And if he started asking questions in a place this small, people would figure he was up to something.

He hoped Needles didn't mind him stalling. After all, he needed to blend in. The aviator sunglasses and jean jacket shouldn't have helped, but it did aid him in preventing people from looking at him for too long. Quite possibly out of embarrassment.

The word 'quaint' crossed his mind. Low street lamps, pots of pansies on the corner of brick sidewalks. All the buildings looked pretty old, maybe from the 1950's or earlier. They took good care of them in the sense that they weren't falling apart, though a couple of them were vacant. Someone was playing a guitar on the street corner. He only seemed to know about four chords, but at least he knew them.

On the other side of a small tent selling assorted cat-shaped tchotchkis was a display of flowers uninhibited by canopy: catching his eye with bright yellows and pinks in the sunlight. The slight tint of his sunglasses made them glow, or… maybe it was the migraine. But he found himself walking past the cat figurines without even feigning interest and towards this bright little spot of color.

The flowers were arranged in little white buckets and tilted at an angle so that they could all be seen. The entire display of them had to be about five feet high and ten feet long, and cascaded in colors so bright that he at first thought them to be fake. But they smelled, some of them too strongly, and when he touched them some of their petals bruised.

No one seemed to be manning the station, which he thought was terribly irresponsible. Someone could make off with the entire thing and he'd be out of luck. He refused to believe that even a small town like this didn't have someone with sticky fingers.

He heard a bell ringing behind the display and saw the shadow of someone coming out of the storefront the flowers were perched against. Reuben ducked behind the cat trinket's tent and pretended to be interested in a painted resin figurine of a tabby playing a double bass.

The photos were pretty blurry and didn't give much detail to the man's face, but if the singular long dreadlock that had escaped his puffy hat and ran down the length of his back were any indication, Reuben was pretty sure he'd found Lou.

Maybe it was the angle, but he didn't look nearly as threatening when he had an arm full of daisies. He looked quietly happy to sit on a little stool and greet people as they walked past his stall. He even looked happy when no one bought anything, or looked at him… or even acknowledged that he existed.

That was kind of sad, but Reuben put it into perspective: if a stranger breezed into a town like this and tried to blend in with the townspeople the way Lou was, it made perfect sense that he wasn't going to be accepted very well. And there was always the chance that one or two of them knew who he was.

In a town only two miles square- if one person knew, then everyone knew.

He ditched the cat tent and positioned himself in a cozy little nook with a view of Lou's perch. All he had to do now was keep his phone out and get a photo of him talking to any one of the dozens of cops that seemed to be pretty much everywhere. It didn't even matter what the context was, it just had to look right.

In fact, it took less than an hour before Reuben saw someone with a shiny badge and a blue uniform heading his way. He got the camera function ready on his phone fired up and was ready to take some photos from his pocket when the cop completely missed the shop and had his eyes fixed on him.

"You got a reason to be here?" Reuben looked at his name tag. Officer Durst.

"No," he said, dropping the phone back into his pocket.

Officer Durst scribbled something into his note-pad, ripped it out, and handed it to him.

"The hell is this?"

"A ticket for loitering." He tipped his angular hat before walking away. "Have a nice day."

Reuben looked at the slip of paper in his hand, trying to decipher the jumble of handwritten letters. What was abundantly clear to him was the number fifty, preceded by a dollar sign. "Who the hell tickets fifty for 'loitering,'" he asked no one. "How is that even a crime," he asked to the same no one.

Officer Durst turned around to address the questions personally, significantly angrier than before, and Reuben hurriedly went elsewhere.

And now that he'd had his little brush with the law, he could see that there were Cops everywhere. This block alone was crawling with them, and they must be bored around here. No wonder they were making him do it instead of pulling from any of the other guys in their pool of resources. Reuben didn't have a criminal record, at least much of one, anyone else would likely have been arrested on the spot.

He angrily stared down at the loitering ticket. How is loitering even a crime in the 21st century? He wadded it up and tossed it against the windshield of his car. He could still see Lou from this spot, but the camera saw him as a barely-moving brownish dot against a butter-yellow backdrop. This was no good. Of course, it meant another day of work, another day of pay- so it wasn't all bad. But it did mean that now he had to strategize: follow him around, maybe get a foot in the door and try to get to know him.

That meant socializing, which was just awful.

The sun began to settle against the bare tops of the trees, casting the street in a reddish color. Tents were dismantled and goods were packed away in rolling totes and put into pickups and minivans.

Reuben had stopped staring at the shop, deciding that it was a futile effort to get anything on him with all the police hanging around. But the sound of car doors slamming and the feeling of lightness when the street cleared broke him out of his seven-hour daze. The smell of dog biscuits still lingered in the air, but he now had a clear view of Lou's shop as he broke down his display. It looked like he hadn't sold much, if anything. The cops had moved on, now that the rest of the town had been ushered back to their homes.

Lou emerged from his shop, carrying a large black bag, and locked the door.

Well, that was certainly interesting. He didn't seem to be going towards any car, but he was definitely going somewhere with that bag. Reuben hadn't given up yet- he was going to find some dirt on the guy some-how and that was certainly a dirty-looking bag he had there.

He kept a generous twenty feet behind Lou as he very casually walked through the brick-paved sidewalk. You could fit anything in a bag that size, he thought. Guns, drugs, money. A dead body.

Well, maybe not a dead body but probably parts of one. Like an entire leg, perhaps.

Maybe a really small dead body.

He spent a good three blocks trying to figure out if there was a dead body in that bag or not. By that time he decided that the bag wasn't moving the right way to be something soft or squishy. Didn't move right for a sack of money, either.

Guns, maybe.

He was judging the weight and movement of the bag so intensely that he didn't notice that they'd run completely out of sidewalk until his shoes started squeaking against wet grass. Finally paying more atten-tion to his surroundings instead of contemplating the contents of a stranger's duffel, he realized that Lou had lead him out into the woods. The sun was almost down completely now, leaving only little hints of red through the trees.

Reuben hid behind a bush, waiting to see what would happen and his camera ready. As the sun disap-peared, a streetlight flickered on and the shadows of three other men walked through it to join Lou.

Well now, this could be anything. But if his experience was worth its salt, it was that strange men meeting in dark places was generally some variety of criminal activity. This weird little burgh didn't have dark alleys. The treeline by the river seemed to be a good enough place to conduct any kind of business.

And Reuben thought, well… if he couldn't get footage of him with a cop, then catching him doing business with someone outside of the family was just as good.

The light was leaving, he'd have to do this quick or suffer the pitfalls of orange street lamp illumination. He saw something round, white before Lou turned away from his line of sight. Damnit. He snapped a couple photos anyhow, thinking maybe it would pick up something better than just his vague outline.

And that was when he heard a steady beat begin. It took him a moment, but soon he realized that the sound was coming from the four of them.

For fuck's sake. He followed the man for almost a mile to snoop on him and a god damned drumming circle. Damn hippies. He bit his tongue and tried to hold back from screaming in frustration.

Twenty minutes of drumming had gone by and it looked like these hippies were set to last the whole night. God-fucking-damnit. There was nothing on this guy.

This was taking too long.

He walked another twenty feet away from the drum circle before dialing 911. "Hello," he said, disguising his voice by an entire octave upward and about thirty years. "Yes, there are some men out in the park making an awful racket. I can hear them all the way down the street! And I think they might be smoking the mari-ju-ana!"

It took five minutes after hanging up before he saw the flashing lights in the distance and that was just about enough time for him to conceal himself behind another bush. The drumming slowed to a stop while the sirens gave a warning 'whoop.' Reuben heard the other three escape through the bushes just as the car doors slammed. He lifted his camera just about an inch above the bushes.

Lou came out from behind the tree-line, illuminated by the street lamps and the flashing red-and-blue of the police car. Damn, that was going to fuck with the light balance. But if the best he was going to get was blurry silhouettes in a night shot, well… honestly it almost added a touch more legitimacy to it.

The cop got out of the car and shared an intense silence with the florist.

"We got a call about a disturbance," the cop said finally.

"This is a public park, you know," Lou said. "I pay my taxes."

"You were being too loud. We have to respond to complaints." The cop put a hand on his radio and mumbled something into it. Click, click, click, went the shutter on the camera. The silence between them was a real, physical thing. The cop sighed. "Lou, I told you to cut down on the weird shit."

"This is one of our holidays and no one's getting hurt over it. We got religious freedom in this country."

It seemed like anything the cop said was going to be a long, drawn-out sigh. "You can't be doing this these days. People around here get a little jumpy about this kinda shit and you gotta tone it the fuck down." The Cop wasn't sounding like a Cop. Click click click. "Look, I'm gonna let you off with a warning. But if I come to hear you doing stuff like this again, you're coming down to the station." Lou bristled and clenched his fists, but said nothing. "Are you hearing me, Lou," the cop demanded.

From his distance, Reuben couldn't even hear if Lou said anything. If it was anything at all, it was little more than a mumble. From behind his bush, the best he could see was a hung head. The cop accepted this and got back into his vehicle.

As he drove away, Lou took a step towards the car and yelled, albeit late: "Yeah, my taxes pay your salary too, Mike." Mike The Cop was already down the road, but Lou seemed pretty pleased with his belated comeback. Nonetheless, he started sagging his shoulders in defeat and gathered his things.

So far this was a waste of time. The photos he'd gotten here were pretty much useless between the obvious animosity that Lou had against the police and the shitty lighting. He gave them a quick glance before the man started walking away from the park. Nothing but silhouettes and tension. Damnit. All he needed was one good photo and he could just coast on it until Needles showed up for a check-in. But even that was proving to be harder than he thought.

His entire walk back to the car, Reuben tried writing scenarios where he might see him cooperating with the police a little more. As someone who barely ever cooperated with anyone, he found it a considerable challenge. Cops, being his least favorite kinds of people, were even less cooperable.

So it became clear to him that to set up anything worth capturing, he was going to have to get to know him better.

Which meant making friends.

The word left a sour taste in his mouth. He was never good at it. How did you make friends as an adult? He couldn't even do that in college, where it was supposed to be easy. Needles and them came to him, not

23

the other way around and to use the word 'friends' to describe their posse was stretching the definition a little too far.

He got back to his car, crawled into the back seat, and called it a night.

A Brief History of Personal Injury

When he awoke, Waving Jesus was joined by a flier for the four-chord guitarist on the corner. He made a considerable amount of effort to make sure that he didn't sleep in and was pleased to discover that he had woken up at ten in the morning. He was absolutely capable of being responsible.

Today was the day. Or rather, today was going to be the first of a few days with a better and more stable plan. He wrestled a bit with clean clothes, managing to pull a miraculous trick of physics to do so while hidden in the back seat of his station wagon. A stray passerby may have noticed the occasional emergence of a naked foot while he struggled to put on pants, rising from behind the panel of the door like an underfed whale and crashing back down as he wriggled them over his hips.

It was clear that this was not the first time he had done this. It was also not the first time that he had trimmed his goatee in the rearview mirror.

The shop was already open by the time Reuben rounded the corner, and had been for awhile. Lou was spending a quiet moment watering the plants, checking their leaves for what Reuben suspected was probably mold. He spent a few moments pondering the simplicity of this man's life, how nice it must be sometimes to have an honest job in a quiet town. To cater to little plants instead of sharp-fingered men and invisible bosses.

Well, at least it was a simple life for now. Reuben was about to ruin it.

His entrance was announced with the ring of a little bell above the door and Lou looked up from inspecting some kind of lily. "Welcome," he said, pushing s dreadlock away from his face. Regardless, it ended up dangling in the way until he stood up. "How can I help you?"

Towering an entire foot over him, Lou was even taller up close than he was from a distance. And Reuben's immediate reaction to someone of considerable height was to be intimidated, given that his usual encounters with taller people are those who threaten violence. But even so, there was something about Lou that just… wasn't intimidating to him. Even if he knew he could probably crush his skull between this two palms, it was hard to imagine him actually doing that here. Maybe it was the gentleness that he spent on his flowers or the minutes-late comeback he'd offered the police last night. Maybe it was because he just… didn't look mean, at least not when he was trying to be friendly.

Oh right. Talking. He had to talk now. Why did people go into florists again? What was the next holiday? … Labor Day?

"I need something for… a funeral," he mumbled. Funerals happened anytime of the year. At least that part wouldn't require too much thinking.

Lou dropped a pair of clippers into his apron pocket and developed a solemn look. "My condolences," he said. Reuben had never met a person this sincere in his entire life. "Who died?"

"My… great aunt… twice removed. She married in, hardly knew her."

He pondered this for a moment. "Well, it's good that you're thinking of her now. What did you know about her?"

Reuben began trying to come up with a good generic description of his deceased fictional relative. "She… hm… she was a very wholesome woman, very no-nonsense. Liked soap operas and cross-stitch."

Lou began picking flowers from their buckets, inspecting a long, white gladiola. "White is a common color for funerals, unless you have any special requests."

"Um… she liked… yellow?"

Lou smiled. "That's a very cheery color. Do you know how much you're willing to spend?"

Spend? If Reuben wasn't careful, this could end up costing him. He hated spending money, particularly on useless things like flowers. Why couldn't this pigeon have been a bartender or something useful?

"Not… too much. I mean, she was removed twice."

"I can do something simple for about thirty dollars," Lou offered helpfully.

Reuben felt a swift punch in the wallet. "Oh, is that all," he said. That was some price gouging right there. He bet he could get it for half the price at the grocery store. Hell, he could go out into the field, pick some weeds, and do the same thing for free. His great aunt twice removed would be rolling around in her grave if she weren't freshly dead and also completely fictional.

But Lou seemed to take that as an affirmative and began arranging them neatly in their decorative wrapping. He managed to somehow take a handful of scrawny-looking flowers and make them look like a hundred. He arranged them artfully in their bundle, arching them almost as though he were making a mockery of Reuben's inability to do it himself.

He wiped away a few stray petals, giving the entire thing a last look before deciding it was finished. "I certainly hope she likes it," he said. Reuben declined to remind him that she was dead and wouldn't be liking much of anything.

Begrudgingly, Reuben reached over the counter for the flower arrangement, still trying to think of a way to weasel out of spending thirty dollars on something that he was literally going to throw out as soon as he got the chance.

The following happened in this order and over the course of three seconds. Out of the corner of his eye, Reuben saw a white truck slow down in front of the store. There was loud crash and he was aware of one of the front windows shattering into millions of pieces. He was not aware of the big, red brick careening towards him- just that his face suddenly hurt and he was on the floor. The faint sound of screeching tires provided a harmony to the ringing in his ears.

When the room stopped spinning, he peeled himself off the floor, but only an inch before rolling back onto his back in pain.

"Jesus Christ, are you okay," Lou asked, though Reuben couldn't do much in the way of answering aside from a moan. Lou began searching frantically for a First Aid kit. "Shit, shit shit," he muttered as he tore through the cabinet to find it. Though, once it was in his hands, he seemed at a loss for what to do with it.

He held up two fingers. "Um… how many fingers am I holding up?"

"Thirty four, now give me the damn ice pack." Without question, Lou tentatively handed the cold pack to him, Reuben promptly slammed it against the floor and dropped it on his face. "Am I bleeding?" Christ, it felt like he was bleeding.

"I'm calling the hospital," he said.

Reuben sat bolt up and immediately regretted it. "No hospitals," he said. Hospitals asked for information. Hospitals were a mess if you were going under an assumed name, which he wasn't yet but he would have to be when he got there. But Lou was looking at him weird. "I mean… It's just a scratch. I can handle it myself."

"Okay, but I am gonna call the police." He turned to speak into his phone.

Reuben's whole body protested the idea of getting the police involved, but once his head cleared a little he began to think of the opportunity to get the shot he had been waiting for. "You'll need a witness," he offered.

This town was so damn small that there was a police vehicle sitting outside the shop in less than a minute. Reuben was honestly a little surprised that his phone call didn't amount to sticking his head out the door and flagging one of them down.

When an officer came, it was not the same one from the previous night. Reuben noticed, but he didn't do much in the way of caring, even though it would not have surprised him to see the same people twice in a period of twenty-four hours.He was preoccupied with getting a good shot of the two of them talking.

The lighting was definitely better here, and if he cropped it just right he could make the cracks in the window look like it was just light refracting.

Lou was keeping a perfect calm as he talked to the cop about what had happened. "I didn't see much," he said. "I was finishing up an order and all of a sudden a brick hits him in the face, glass is everywhere."

"It... it was a white truck," Reuben offered. "Didn't see much else. Before... y'know... the brick hit my face."

Well, some witness he made. Lou seemed unimpressed with his input but didn't ask him to leave. Having him present offered a little bit more legitimacy than if it were just Lou claiming it. It became clear to Reuben that for as much of a marshmallow as Lou was, he was not well-liked for one reason or another in this town.

"Everyone in this town has a white or silver car," said the officer. "Except for the station wagon parked at the minimart." Reuben narrowed his eyes. He was going to have to move his car. "Do you need to go to the hospital, sir?"

"I'm... fine," he said crossly, holding the ice pack firmly to his face. "It's... just a bruise."

"Sir, you're bleeding from a head-wound."

"I've got a band-aid," he said.

The officer looked as though he was about to protest the effectiveness of a band-aid against head-trauma, but decided that it wasn't worth it. "We'll put out an APB for someone in a white car with a brick," he said, laughing. "Until then, get a tarp or something to cover up that window."

Lou nodded. The cop left. Reuben let his shoulders drop, realizing that the process of hiding his face behind the cold pack had wound a significant knot in his shoulder. And now that he wasn't standing up out of sheer determination, he sank back down against the wall. He thought that the loud 'thunk' against the wall would have caught the shop-owner's attention, but Lou's eyes were forward and staring at nothing. His lips were moving, repeating the same words over and over again.

"Don't get mad," he said in a nearly inaudible mumble. "Don't get mad, don't get mad…"

Lou's shoulders slowly drooped, though he was far from relaxed. His fists were clenching and unclenching as he surveyed the bulk of the damage. He kicked idly at a shard of broken glass. Reuben was waiting for him to lash out, do something violent like he would expect someone in his position to do, but it was as though all of the shaking anger in him left his body with a single, audible breath.

"Are you able to stand," he asked, taking a couple steps towards the damage. "There's a bathroom in the back," Lou said while rearranging the lilies in the window so he could clear away the glass. "Clean the blood off your face."

"Yeah," he said, trying to get back to his feet. He had to climb the wall with his palms to get himself upright, and didn't let go of it until he found the bathroom.

In terms of criminal activity, money laundering is relatively safe. You get a bag of money, you get rid of a bag of money, no one has to talk to each other. When it came to tailing people, that was another pretty safe job because there was a considerable amount of distance between him and the person who was actually going to get his ass kicked.

So after doing this for a whole five years without injury or incident and the very first time he gets something that might leave a scar, it was from a god-damned brick that wasn't even aimed at him.

The cut wasn't very big, but man- it looked like he was trying to fellate a baseball. It had hit him flat against the cheekbone, and a line of blood was trickling down the side of his forehead. He wasn't sure if his teeth were loose or if they just felt that way because of some psychology bullshit, but something inside his mouth felt askew. Maybe it was his jaw. It could have been knocked out of place or something.

A doctor would probably know the answer to all of these inquiries, however… Reuben was just fine.

He ran the water and peered through the crack in the door. Lou was busy trying to cover up the hole in his storefront. While he wasn't looking, he swiped through the photos he'd taken. They were good enough, he thought. If he cropped them right it would look like it was just the two of them talking. Unlike the photos taken last night, Lou didn't seem angry. He just seemed…

Sad.

Reuben could leave. He'd gotten his shots in, he could probably go home.

But maybe it was the long look that Lou was giving the shattered glass on the floor or maybe it was the way that all the flowers in the shop seemed to be wilting, or it could have easily been the concussion, but he couldn't just leave the poor guy here to stew in defeat. Besides, every extra day he spent with him was another grand in his wallet and another chance for better photos- especially if this investigation was ongoing.

Hmm… sad wouldn't do. He needed to stick around and see this resolved and maybe get the bastard to smile in one of the photos. In the meantime, he'd have to stay pretty close to Lou just in case

"Hey man," he said, dabbing the cut on his forehead with a wet rag. "It's been a rough day. You... wanna get a drink or something?"

Lou lifted his head, twirling a white lily from the now ruined floral arrangement between his fingers. "I have to cover up the window," he said.

"So we'll cover up the window and then get a drink."

Lou looked at the jagged teeth and gaping maw left in the window and sank into himself. "It's not even noon."

"I bet by the time we finish cleaning this place up, it'll be at least two."

Lou gave an exhausted kind of laugh. "He's got jokes." Reuben wasn't about to tell him that he wasn't joking since it at least got him to crack a smile. "Alright, Funny-bone. I got some duct tape and a tarp in the closet. How's your head?"

Reuben gingerly touched the skin where the corner of the brick hit his face. The bleeding had stopped and the worst he felt was dizzy. Granted, drinking alcohol may not be the smartest of ideas after getting in hit in the head with a brick, but he had a habit of saying: 'if you can't fix it, drink.'

Of course, he was only on record as saying this aloud once.

"I'll be fine," he said. "So, know any good places around here?"

Lou shook his head. "Only one that I'm comfortable going to."

We get it, Lou. You're kind of weird and people don't like you a lot. Otherwise they wouldn't be throwing bricks into your windows. But come on, it can't be

33

that bad.

But whatever. If it was going to get him some-where with people and good lighting, he would gladly let him pick whatever bar he wanted to go to. Lou descended from the display riser and sighed deeply at his job well done. "You know," he said. "A beer does sound pretty good right now."

"That's the spirit," Reuben said, laughing at his own pun.

Lou looked at him with concern. "Are you… sure you should be drinking? You did get hit in the head."

"With a brick," Reuben offered helpfully.

"With a brick," Lou agreed. Reuben wobbled slightly. "Maybe I should drive."

You never know what to expect when someone says that their watering hole of choice is 'out a ways.' Is it a sports bar? Is it one of those hipster joints? Well, the name of the place was 'Barnaby's' which could have meant literally anything. It was a little brick building squashed between two other brick buildings, with a little blue awning and umbrellas on the patio.

They arrived by way of Lou's old Volvo, which smelled like it needed an oil change. Reuben, distracting himself from his discomfort of being driven around by anyone but himself, silently counted six bars on the five minute drive, but no- Lou just had to go to this one.

To get to the front door you had to park in the back, walk through some narrow alley, around the fence enclosing the patio, and then through the patio itself. He couldn't help but think that there were easier ways to design a layout.

After walking through the doorway, he was still

unclear what kind of bar this was. The place had low ceilings and brick walls, not that you could tell what the walls were made of under all the junk they had adhered to it. It wasn't the usual kind of junk. The usual kind of junk was photos of sports teams, signed jerseys, photos of famous people. Reuben was greeted by someone's crude scrawling of a cuttlefish on a post-it note.

The contents of the walls were all similarly decorated with odd junk that could have been the life's work of a hermit. There was a tricycle mounted on the far end of the building. Christmas lights were woven into the spokes of the wheel and it was being used as a light fixture.

There was a stage. Well, no- it wasn't a stage. There was a sunken floor where all the tables were, sparsely populated with people. The 'stage' was on the other side of it, just a little nook where the floor no longer sank. What made it a stage was a microphone and someone speaking into it.

Was that… was that poetry? It just sounded like words, in his opinion. None of it rhymed and it sort of had a rhythm to it, he supposed, but he was just not getting anything from it. That was going to be a distraction. He didn't care much for sports unless there was a pool going and even when that was happening he tuned out the majority of the noise. But this was going to be harder to ignore, especially with the way the sound got muffled by all the shit on the walls.

Lou lead him to a bar stool near the corner of the bar and let him take his seat before taking his own. The bartender, a twenty-something with blue streaks in her hair, saw Lou first and only passively seemed to notice Reuben.

"S'been awhile, Lou," she said. "Your usual?"

Lou gave Reuben a look of consideration. "I think I've decided on coffee tonight," he said.

"Your loss," she said. "Dude, what happened to your face," she said to Reuben, when she finally decided to notice him.

"You should see the other guy," Reuben said proudly.

"The other guy is a brick," Lou said. "I'd rather not get into it. Coffee for me and… um…"

"You know, I think I'm feeling a gin and tonic." The bartender gave him a skeptical look. "What, you DO have those things here, right?" He would be the type who took people to bars that only served specialty drinks. Did he have to say the code word?

Lou made a low gesture with his left hand, almost out of Reuben's range of sight. Reuben's mouth twitched a little.

"Yeah, I can do that for you," she said.

Reuben's drink was ready long before Lou's, and by the time Lou had a mug in his hand Reuben had already downed half of his tumbler. "So," he said. "Why are people throwing bricks at me?"

"They aren't. They threw a brick at me and missed."

"Okay, but why?"

Lou sighed. "I'm sure they have their reasons."

"I'll tell you why someone might throw a brick at me," Reuben offered. Lou turned his head. "It would be because I ripped them off."

"That's kinda rude," he said.

"Well, it's kind of the nature of the business," he explained. "I run a pawn shop."

"Pawn shop," Lou asked. "I don't think we have one of those around here. But… I guess you're just here for the funeral, aren't you?"

"The- oh. Yes. My great aunt. Whom I will miss greatly."

"Despite not being fond of her?"

"Uh… distance makes the heart grow fonder."

"Dude, are you feeling alright?"

He had been trying to ignore just how fast the room had been spinning. He'd found himself trying to focus several times but unable to see anything more solid than the trails of lights left by the tricycle on the wall. Lou's face was an incohesive blur. The gin had hit him harder than he'd thought it would.

And there was that thought in the back of his mind, in a jumbled mess of thoughts and ideas. Insisting on a barely-attended bar. The hand gestures when he ordered his drink, don't think for a minute he didn't see them. Who orders coffee?

It was a setup. Lou must have known why he was here. They put something in his drink.

He needed to move, and fast. His feet felt like lead and they tangled in the legs of the stool. Shit, he should have seen this coming. He should have seen this coming, he should have seen this coming, he should have-

All the way down, into darkness.

The dullest of thuds echoed in his head.

The best part of waking up

Reuben's first thought when he woke up was to check to see if he still had his kidneys, which would be very notable thought if it weren't something of a habit whenever he awoke in a place that was not his own bed or the back seat of his car. However, the thought came first. The actual action of opening his eyes to see where exactly he was… took more time.

Well, it didn't feel like a bathtub full of ice. That was a good start. Or a bad one. If they took his kidneys and just left him there, well…

No wait, he'd be dead.

This was comfy. Death was comfy.

No searing pain in his sides. He did have a raging headache, though. And every muscle that he tried to move ached like hell.

He made a conscious decision to open his eyes.

The light in the room was warm, something like dawn. The place smelled like dirt and dust and cigarette smoke stuck in the peeling paint of the walls. Somewhere above his head, there were a series of brown things hanging from the ceiling. After some effort to focus, it became clear that they were the bottoms of hanging planters.

It became very clear to him that he'd been drugged and then taken to Lou's house and that didn't sit well with him. He started a full-body panic, but with as sore as he was his escape attempt amounted to a series of poorly-controlled shakes.

A rustle to his right and he heard a voice. A woman's, to his surprise, and full of ennui. "Lou, your friend's awake," she said.

Reuben shifted his head so that he could see. She was leaning back in an ugly brown chair, one leg dangling over the upholstered arm. She didn't even bother looking at him, her magazine was more important. Blonde hair fell over her face in a soft arch, twirling it in her dark blue fingernails.

But all of this seemed secondary to the fact that she wasn't wearing a bra.

Oh, sure: she was wearing a dark-colored top, but Reuben could always tell. They weren't particularly big, but there's a way that a woman holds herself when she isn't wearing a bra. Like she's stopped giving a crap about it half a decade ago.

This wasn't how he had expected to wake up, but well… he wasn't exactly complaining at the moment. Temporarily forgetting the distress of waking up in a strange place and possibly being drugged, he ventured an attempt to sit up and introduce himself properly, but was thrown back by a throbbing pain in his head.

"Slow down there, slick," she said, deeply unconcerned with whether he was going to take her advice.

He was on a couch in a large room, which he would tentatively call a 'living room' except that it seemed to share space with a small dining room as well. The dining room was also attached to the kitchen and the only real thing separating any of these rooms was a large, circular white table.

Lou appeared from around the corner, phone

in hand. Reuben's demeanor immediately sank as the woman pried herself off the chair and Lou came closer.

The lingering sense of paranoia made Reuben press himself against the back of the couch to get away from him. Regret filled him when the action revealed a wave of stiffness and soreness encompassing his whole body. He could feel something like a bruise on his shoulder, as though he'd been dropped on it more than once.

"What the hell did you do to me," he demanded, though with as dry as his throat was it wasn't much of a demand.

Lou looked mildly hurt by the accusation, but shrugged it off as one of a thousand others. "You were pretty stubborn about not going to a hospital," he said. "I had Jane stitch you up. She was pre-med at one point."

"You put something in my drink," Reuben accused weakly. It was intended to be a shout but the sudden movement knocked the wind out of him.

"I… what?"

"You drugged me!" Lou opened his mouth to speak, but his words failed him. The best he could manage was a baffled 'eh?' "Don't you try to play innocent on me, buddy. I know what happened!" Reuben began going into a coughing fit from his dry throat, not that this stopped him from making accusatory gestures in Lou's general direction.

Lou was slow to respond, not quite sure what to make of the implication. "You think that I put something in your drink."

"I don't think, dude. I know."

"You think that I put something in your drink so I could drag your skinny ass across town and… tuck

41

you in?"

Reuben narrowed his eyes, but was now incredibly conscious of the fact that he was comfortably underneath layers of blankets. Not the usual protocol, that was for sure. That is to say... what protocol there was for this kind of situation. Which, he supposed, there wasn't any.

He raised an eyebrow, waiting for an explanation.

Lou sighed and collapsed into the brown chair. "You know, going out for drinks so soon after a serious head injury has to be the dumbest suggestion I've ever seen a grown man make. It's probably a good thing you wouldn't weigh more than stone fifty soaking wet."

"I said I was fine."

"You collapsed halfway through the world's lightest gin and tonic. You were *not fine.*" Lou took a deep breath, no doubt repeating his mantra of *don't get mad, don't get mad... Breath in, two three, out two three.* "But it looks like you're better, at least." He shook his head. "Is this something that you just... do? Have a drink every time someone hits you in the head with a rock?"

"It's a pretty good way to forget that you've gotten hit in the head with a rock." He lifted a hand to his face. The swelling was down, but there was definitely a ridge along the side of his forehead where he'd been sewn back up. Pre-med, huh? Probably looked like a toddler did it.

Lou withheld his commentary. "Well, I guess you'll be missing that funeral," he said.

"The what?"

"The... funeral? The reason why you're here?"

"Right, my uncle."

"I thought it was your aunt."

"Aunt-uncle. Bi-gender."

"Well, either way- there's only one funeral happening today and it started about fifteen minutes ago."

Any time Reuben could gracefully let himself out of a lie it was like someone opened a window in a stuffy room. He let out a breath that he'd been holding in for the entirety of their meeting, and hoped that it came across as a sigh of grief for his dead aunt-uncle. He slouched against the cushions of the futon, sinking back into the mattress pad. "I… guess I came all this way for nothing," he said.

"Well, I wouldn't trust you behind the wheel of anything for awhile. Jane says you might have some dizzy spells and stuff for the next few days, so you might as well stick around before you go home." He sat forward and got to his feet, shaking something invisible from his shoulders. "I have to go talk to someone about that window. I'll have Jane keep an eye on you, just take it easy, okay?"

Reuben nodded, though 'easy' was not going to be the way things go when his legs felt like limp noodles and he had an assignment to do that required him to not be on a stranger's couch. Before Lou disappeared around the corner, he knocked softly on the door to the next room.

The walls here were thin enough that he could hear the conversation with Jane. "Hey, could you keep an eye on him," he asked. "Like just in case he passes out again."

"Sure, whatever," she said. Damn, he could hear everything. Any snooping around he did was going to have to be really careful. Provided that she cared, of course- which seemed unlikely.

The door locked behind Lou and he gave it a good minute after he heard the engine of his car start, just in case she decided to check on him then and there. A minute passed and nothing happened. Her bedside manner was awful.

Reuben slowly bent his knees, trying to work life back into his muscles. He couldn't believe that he passed out after one drink. That had to be an exaggeration.

He heard just about every vertebrae pop back into place as he slowly sat upright. A couch was better than the backseat of the car, but only in the sense that it was intended to laid down on and didn't have a fossilized french fry wedged between the cushions. It was not, however, a place intended for a good night's sleep.

Which he wouldn't have gotten anyway.

Lou wasn't joking about the dizziness. Even just sitting up made the room spin and he held onto the edge of the cushion as though that was going to somehow prevent him from toppling over.

After a few moments of breathing steadily and the room equalized. He was *fine.* More important than fine, he had work to do. There was money to be made.

Lou seemed to take his work home with him in the sense that it wasn't just the one or two hanging potted plants that decorated the window. There was no shortage of greenery, much of it set into little window boxes nailed into the wall and each of them illuminated by a spectrum lamp. He spotted at least three different kinds of cacti, none of which he knew the names for. The only reason he recognized the spider plant on the opposite wall was because he once, in a mood to improve his life, bought one to live in the bathroom.

For a plant that's supposed to be able to outlive

the worst conditions, he sure did manage to kill it pretty fast.

Apart from that, it didn't look like the hippy hide-away that he'd imagined. Not that he was actively imagining what kind of a place Lou would live in, but he was suspecting more tye-die. The air was curiously absent of the scent of patchouli oil and nothing seemed Buddha-shaped.

For all he saw of the living room, the place looked clean and modern.

What even was this guy?

Well, he was about to go and find out.

He limped stiffly away from the futon, holding onto the edges of end tables and walls for support and knocking over a succulent in the process. See, he was fine. He just needed to work his legs back into moving again, no big deal. He could use this to his advantage: he could essentially play dead and spend a considerable amount of time snooping around. This head wound was a blessing in disguise.

To his right, a hallway that included Jane's room. To his left, a kitchen, some kind of study. There was no guarantee that he would find any dirt on Lou in either direction, but if Reuben surmised that if he had a secret he'd be keeping it in his bedroom.

Lou's room shared a wall with Jane's. At least, he assumed it was Lou's room.

The amount of greenery tripled here, which was amazing considering that his bedroom was barely half the size of the living room. He could fit a bed against the window and that took up the entire back wall. He could only imagine that he had to walk sideways to get to it.

Potted plants hung from the curtain rod, four of

them at different heights. With the possible exception of the bed, every conceivable surface had something green and living arranged on it. Otherwise, it was pretty sparse: a dresser against the wall, a desk, and a chair. This was a room used mostly for sleeping and not much else.

There was so much junk on the dresser that he had to focus on what was and was not important. He had an entire shelf dedicated to potted succulents, and some kind of crawling vine starting to overcrowd the pot on the shelf below it. Little wood carvings of animals were each set against the back of a desk, facing in towards the room. Their painted black eyes seemed like they might be staring at him.

Reuben picked one of them up- a raccoon. It wasn't well-carved, to be frank. It looked like it had been done with a pocket-knife. He supposed that the only way he knew it was a raccoon was the fact that they'd stained a mask over his eyes.

It was a stupid little knick-knack. The weirdo probably thought it was magic or something.

What was curiously missing from what Reuben imagined would be in Lou's apartment was anything that could conceivably be used as a bong or even one single Bob Marley poster; disappointing. He was actually kind of pissed about it, to be honest. You think you'd know a guy after talking to him for twenty minutes.

He put the raccoon down, trying to match the dust spots as well as he could. He vaguely recognized some of the surrounding figures: a wolf, some kind of cat, a snake. The rest were kind of vague quadrupeds. Camels? Horses? Cows? Hell if he knew. It didn't seem that important, anyhow. There wasn't any hard information from this diorama other than the fact that Lou was weird and liked animals.

He could hear Jane speaking softly to someone on the other side of the wall… just how many people lived here, anyways?

And then… a rhythmic thumping sound. It didn't take long for Reuben to realize what was going on, particularly when she started moaning.

Was she... was she masturbating? Really? When you've got guests in the house? And damn, she was loud.

Loud enough that she probably wouldn't hear him moving around. He tested the waters by opening one of the drawers in the desk. The drawer squeaked upon opening and there was no change from the thump-thump-thump and one-sided-grunts and the… heavy breathing and…

No, he had to focus. He had to not think about the woman on the other side of the wall, who didn't seem to give a crap about bras or guests… naked and sweating and wondering if she… used her fingers or…

Baseball scores were traditional, of course, but baseball always made Reuben think of betting, and thoughts of money and gambling did nothing to keep the blood from rising and his toes from curling and…

Focus on the goal. Find out as much as he can about this guy and hand him over to Needles. Make money. The girl in the next room was too young for him anyhow, but damn if he wasn't thinking about the color of her cheeks and…

He was dizzy. Holy hell, all that effort just to get himself sitting upright. No, he could do this. He could do this. He would just have to… steady himself. The more he moved, the more he would get used to the dizziness. Just keep moving… stop thinking about Jane.

He could lay back down when he got a chance.

Thump-thump-thump…

When he looked down, he saw the corner of a red and white international mailing envelope sticking out of the drawer. Well, that was certainly inviting. He flipped the drawer open with his foot and it was full of mail. Who keeps letters in this day and age, he thought. Who even sends them?

The return address for one of them was a PO Box in Kumasi, Ghana. This was the kind of dirt he was looking for. Deals overseas. Maybe weapons, maybe drugs. It didn't matter. He took a couple snapshots of the address, struggling to keep the camera's focus. He shut the drawer as soon as he got something clear enough to send.

Jane was climaxing in the next room. He could tell by the frequency of the thumping noise and the pitch of her screams. His hands shook at the thought and he bit his lip trying to keep his mind from wandering, but it wasn't doing any god-damned good. Blood that should have been keeping him upright went…well, elsewhere and his knees began to bend.

Very clearly, he was not fine.

His knees hit the floor and the room was spinning. The noise was a thunderous 'thud' against the carpet and he scrambled to get back to the door. But the most he could manage was to drape an arm over the side of a rolling chair and wait for the room to stop moving underneath him.

The sharp scent of cigarette smoke stung his nose and the room went quiet, but for a soft murmur. He sank his head into the corner of the seat cushion and made a sad little sound of frustration as he tried to shake the image from his head and find his feet. Neither seemed to work.

The smell of smoke got stronger and he lifted his head. Jane was standing at the entrance of the room, cigarette between her lips and wiping her fingers off with a paper towel. Oh god, she really was using her fingers. His head felt heavy and his chest felt weak. He couldn't feel his legs at all, but for a faint static and an ache.

"The hell is wrong with you," she said from the side of her mouth. She was wrapped in a short, black bathrobe that only came down to her mid-thigh. Her short hair was no longer artfully swept to the side but now tangled in the back and he thought of... hair-pulling. A trail of smoke escaped from her lips and all he could think of was how red they were. She was still not wearing a bra, of this he was certain.

Was she dripping down her leg or...

"Bathroom," he said.

"That way," she said, pointing down the hall. "I'd help you get there, but Lou's got a thing about smoking in his room. Guess you're on your own."

Her's was a cruel smile.

Speak softly and carry a big secret.

Lou's arrival was marked with the loud steps made by walking through a foyer too small to house him. Reuben heard him before he saw him, which offered him enough time to look like he had been sleeping instead of quietly trying to snoop around between dizzy spells.

Jane had left, soon becoming bored with the task of taking care of him. It wasn't like she brought him home in the first place, he shouldn't be her responsibility. This left him free to explore Lou's room, only to come up mostly empty-handed with the exception of a few old envelopes from various countries in Africa, emptied. Kind of stupid of him to leave that kind of thing just laying around where anyone could find it, but he wasn't about to complain. It wasn't much of a find, but anything that would help them put the pieces together would be more money in his pocket.

That is to say, when he could stay upright for more than five minutes at a time. He couldn't imagine that the sudden rush had helped. Christ, this place needed sound-proofing.

Lou came in to check on Reuben almost immediately.

"How's your head doing," he asked. Lou looked worse for the wear, to be honest. Tired, and unhappy did not wear well on his face.

"How's the window," Reuben countered.

51

Lou smiled briefly at the question. Making this about him instead of Reuben's swirling head seemed to be at least one way to get him to warm up. But the smile lasted a short time before it turned into a sigh. "The odd shape of the frame is going to mean getting a custom cut. Which is expensive, and in the meantime I will have to close the shop. A lot of work is going to go to waste."

"But you can make that back, right?" Lou gave a sad shake of the head. "Oh come on, man. Your profit margin has got to be like 100% if you're selling stuff from your garden."

Lou's sad look worsened. Was it something he'd said?

"I keep forgetting that you're not from around here," he said. "I have to order most of my stock from down the mountain. I actually take a pretty big hit most weeks."

"Still, wouldn't it just be cheaper to grow it yourself and sell it?"

"You can't really... grow much around here," Lou said. "Mining towns aren't noted for their good soil chemistry. I don't have the kind of cash for pH treatments, and there's no guarantee that they'll work. Pretty much everything around here is dead, unless you've got some money to throw at it."

Well, this was getting too technical for Reuben to have any input. But he didn't like not having the last word, so he chose his last words to be flattery. "Well, I'm sure you'll make it back somehow. You're pretty smart, for a guy that doesn't know how to use a cold pack."

Just how great a comfort that was became plain on Lou's face. "You pretty sure I didn't drug you, then?"

The thoughts he'd had upon waking were not much more than a blur now and he'd almost forgotten."What? Dude, I was kidding. Lighten up." Lou did not seem to be much in the mood for lightening anything. "Look, your shop's gonna be fine. Bet you in like... two weeks that window is going to be the least of your worries."

Lou shook his head again. "Many of those flowers need a controlled environment or they'll wilt. I don't have a place here to keep them the right temperature." He sighed. "No matter how I do this, I'm losing money."

He'd just said Reuben's favorite word: 'money.' When preceded by the word 'losing,' it was like feeling his heart jump. "No," he said. "I am not accepting that answer." He sat up, regretted it, and sank back down against the couch. "A guy like you has got to have something up his sleeve."

"Guy like me, huh," he said. "You've known me for one day. What's a guy like me?"

"Well... an honest one," Reuben said. "... a resourceful one, probably." If he could get the guy to admit who he was, this was going to be easier. But not on day two.

"An honest one," he repeated. "That's a good one." There was a buzzing noise and for a moment Reuben thought maybe Jane had left her vibrator on. It became evident that it was not when Lou reached into his pocket and produced a phone. He let out a dismissive groan. "I have to go take care of something," he said. "Just try not to hurt yourself."

And just like that, he was heading back outside. There was no way in hell that he was going to lay around while his target was doing mysterious things in the middle of the night. He got to his feet and limped towards the door, shaking the stiffness from his knees and cracking the joints in his shoulders.

He kept a good distance, making sure that Lou was always a few yards ahead of him and hiding behind something any time he turned his head. This area was different. The quaintness of downtown had given way to some houses that seemed to have been built in a hurry, and he was heading away from it still- into the line of trees that his little brick home was set into. He almost disappeared into the half-dead bushes that marked the end of his property.

Well, if this didn't just reek of something suspicious…

Reuben hurried to keep an eye on him before he disappeared into the woods. He could get closer here without being seen, but if he stepped wrong he might end up cracking a twig.

Not that this was any kind of worry for Reuben. He was good at sneaking around. You had to be good at sneaking around in this line of business, even if you were doing the safe work like money laundering and not talking too loud about it.

The further into the woods he followed, the darker it got, and soon the only way Reuben could navigate was the sound of Lou's footsteps on dead leaves and the beam of his flashlight when he could see it. So when Lou turned his light abruptly off, Reuben froze- thinking that somehow he'd been found.

The darkness was cut suddenly by a yellow light- a lighter. The fire slowly grew, igniting what Reuben registered to be some dry wood in a fire pit about five feet in circumference and elevated two feet off the ground by a stone pedestal. As the flames reached an equilibrium, Reuben began to understand the space he was in.

He was sheltered behind a ring of trees that looked like they could be the only things in this place that were not dead. Their trunks were thicker than he was and the bark of them was starting to flake off, so they weren't completely not-dead. But they seemed as though they had been planted with a purpose, with as perfect a circle they made there was no way that this could have been natural, and even if everything else was bare and dying- these at least had leaves.

Within the circle of trees was a circle of stones, some which were starting to be swallowed by the trunks. The entire place looked like a wall of stone and earth and wood. Reuben wasn't sure what to think of it.

Lou moved around, not much more than a shadow in this dim light. He had tossed something like a heavy black sheet over his shoulders, wrapped it around him until he just looked like one big, black monolith. He had shaken his hair loose from his hat and dreadlocks trailed down this formless garb past his elbows.

The final piece to this ridiculous costume was a gleaming white animal skull that covered his face.

Someone was approaching, he could see him coming through the trees at a hesitant pace, washed in the yellow light of the fire. It was as if the thin man in dirty jeans and plaid wasn't so sure about meeting a florist covered in some ceremonial garb in the middle of the woods.

Lou turned to see the man, who stopped in his tracks and gave every impression of having second thoughts.

"I understand you have a problem," Lou said.

His voice seemed different. It wasn't meek or sad or defeated. It echoed, it boomed. It owned this little circle of trees and the rocks and the fire, it came from the earth, resonating in Reuben's head like thunder.

The stranger nodded. "Nothing will grow," he said, his voice rattling. He toyed with a burlap satchel about the size of his hand. "I've tried everything, but none of them will seed. I'm at my last leg."

"Let me see it," Lou said, holding out a palm. The man began to hand the satchel over, but paused. He looked like he was about to run. "Let me see it," he repeated, unchanging.

The stranger's hands were quick as a flash, handing it to him as if avoiding contact with him as much as possible. Lou emptied the contents into his palm- something brown and loose. He studied it, sifting it through his fingers, setting it on his tongue. Reuben withheld a gag- you don't just stick mystery substances in your mouth like that!

"The soil is… broken," he said. He literally just stuck dirt in his mouth. Was he insane? "Tired."

"Please, tell me what I can do to fix it!"

"There is nothing I can do for this season. This is a rest that takes time."

"What can I do? If we can't grow anything, we'll starve!"

He sifted some of the grains between his fingers. "Burn the wood of an oak tree down until its ashes are white. Burn enough to cover your fields and till it before the frost. Plant your seeds in spring."

"But what will I do until then? Summer is ending and we've got nothing!"

"A year of sacrifice is necessary to start again. We come from the soil, we become the soil, therefore we must share its pain." It was like Lou was a completely different person, waxing poetic about literal dirt.

He paused, the man staring at him. His voice became softer for a moment, more… human. "And for future reference, stop watering your field so much. You're drowning it."

The man nodded gravely and bowed, backing away from Lou for a considerable distance- as if he might change his mind somehow- before running back into the trees. Lou stood still for a moment, making sure he was really gone. From the distance behind his tree, Reuben could hear him chuckling quietly.

He wasn't entirely sure what was going on here, but he knew that he had to get back to the apartment before… before…

….all that running caught up to him. Man, he didn't think it would wind him as badly as it did but suddenly his head was spinning again. He tried to step quietly away and get a head start before Lou saw him, but the sound of leaves crunched in his ears. Focus damnit, focus… get away before…

Lou's head turned, the light of the fire catching a pair of reflectors sewn into the eye sockets of the skull. Reuben pushed himself to run, but he heard the crunching of leaves behind him. Someone grabbed him by the collar of his shirt and pulled him back towards the circle.

"What the fuck do you think you're doing," said Jane. She pulled him back, throwing him back against one of the shedding trees. As soon as she loosened her grip on him he tried running again, but she just grabbed him again and kept him there.

He noticed that she'd ditched the silky robe for black jeans and a black tee. Her hair poked out of a black knit beanie. Of course, it made sense that if she was intent on skulking around in the dark that she'd choose more appropriate attire, but he could always hold out hope. This place was certainly weird enough that someone might be wandering around in the woods in their pajamas.

Oh, she was angry. And he was not in any position to fight back when he couldn't even see straight. And he thought, maybe he could play the concussion card. He was disoriented, he didn't know what he was doing, just started following. But before he could form the words 'where am I' with his mouth, Lou's voice resonated through the trees.

"I can see you," he said. Shit. "Look, dude. You can come out, let me explain."

Jane threw him through the trees with a surprising amount of force. He tumbled into the firelight, followed by Jane- who looked like she wasn't afraid to give him a beating for intruding on… whatever this was.

"We can't just let him run around telling everyone what you're doing," she said.

"Me?" Reuben put a hand to his chest, mock-offended by the suggestion. "I wouldn't tell a soul!"

"I met you this morning, and I already don't believe a word of that." She pushed him to the ground. They both loomed over him as they came closer and he was overcome with a massive sense of dread. He crawled backwards, scrambling to get back to his feet but even if he did find his legs they were weak… and he didn't know how to get back towards town. He was either going to have to talk his way out of this, or head for the hills.

Either decision was making a massive chance.

"Do you want me to kill him? It's okay to say yes."

"Jane, would you chill for a second," Lou said, taking the skull off his head. He shook his locs loose and then tied them back behind him.

One of Reuben's flaws, which perched precariously atop a pile of other flaws, was that his primary response to a tough situation was deeply rooted in sarcasm.

"Either this is one of those weird LARP things the kids do these days or you're conning these hill folk into thinking you're some kind of forest creature that grants wishes."

"I'm not… conning them," he said. "And its more like a…" Lou made a series of unsure hand gestures. "Local god. Part-time."

"Pretending to be a weird god isn't a con… how?"

Lou sighed, removing the rags from his shoulders. He couldn't tell what that emotion was on his face but it wasn't proud of himself. "If they believe that I have the power to make things grow, and if taking my advice gives them the results they need, can I say that it's really pretending?"

Reuben posed himself to say something, but found himself to be without words. He lifted a finger to signify that he would have a proper response upon further contemplation, but when his thoughts came to him, all he could say was:

"Oh, you're good." Lou seemed unamused by the implication, but that didn't stop Reuben from showering him with praise. "You're very good. Its weasel words like that that keep a guy from getting killed. So how do I get in on this?"

"In on what?"

"Well, I know your secret identity so how about you give me a cut of whatever the village people are paying you?"

Lou paused. "They're not paying me anything," he said. Reuben made a sound of disbelief. "The people here need help. They've been living on this land for generations, but it doesn't yield anything anymore. They would rather believe that they are being punished by an old god than that bad things happen for no good reason. I just want to give them what they need."

"And… you're not getting paid for this."

"Some people leave out bread." Lou shrugged

"You get breadcrumbs."

"Well… when you put it that way…"

Reuben shook his head. "You cannot be doing this for free," he said. "You just did some voodoo shit on that guy's lawn. I'd wanna get paid."

Lou's mouth swished to the side of his face. "I dunno, man. I don't even know where I'd start."

"You let me hammer out the details of this… what do you even call this-"

"Krikadoo," Lou said.

"Right. Kickapoo. Listen, I'm a whiz at making money off of things. You just gotta tell me all you know about it and I'll do the rest.

Lou turned his head to the side, as if the answer to his decision was twenty feet to his left. He was thinking about windows. "And you'd want a cut."

"Eighty percent, naturally."

"Eighty." The number seemed sour. "Because you gave me the idea."

"Exactly."

"Seventy," Jane offered. "Seventy for him and I

get a share."

"What," Reuben exclaimed, hurt by the implication that he could be haggled with.

"Jane, you're not helping," Lou whispered.

"Dude, we need the money. That, and I'm bored." She turned back to Reuben, arms crossed. "Lou's the one doing all the work here and I need something to supplement the camgirl business."

Camgirl! Well, now all that made a ton of sense. "Sixty for me, forty between the two of you."

"There is no way I'm walking away from this with twenty percent. When you're sixty percent dirt god, maybe. But just for that, you get twenty."

Reuben gritted his teeth. "For twenty, you can do this on your own and forget about my plan." He hesitated to say it, and when the word came out of his mouth it was through the tiny space between his teeth and his bottom lip. "Thirty-three, three way even split. You can take the decimal points and give them to charity or something."

"I think we have deal," Jane said, after thinking about it for a moment. "So tell me this plan of yours."

"First things first, we need to get more people to believe in him." Jane snorted. "I'm not talking these hill people out here, we need to get some of your hipster friends roped in. Maybe some of people living in-town, too."

"That would make sense if they were farmers," Lou said. "But apart from those little windowsill herb gardens I don't think the Krikadoo can help them."

"Oh, we're not talking about helping anyone," Reuben said. "Except ourselves. So we make him a little more than a dirt god. Walking around with that mask on your head doesn't exactly give off benevolent

61

vibes. People are going to be scared of him, so we make him more threatening."

Lou made a thinking face, which was a slow curl of a wide lower lip and his thick eyebrows almost meeting in the middle. He didn't seem to like that idea very much and Reuben could see why- if you saw the man on the street and didn't know that he had the personality of a Golden Retriever, you'd already think he was scary and intimidating.

"The next thing, once we have enough people believing this thing isn't just some Scooby-Doo villain, is make sure that they know it isn't you."

"But… it is me."

"No," Reuben said. "It's not."

"But… I…" The concept finally clicked. "Oh. Gotcha."

Reuben was beginning to think that the reason Lou had strayed from The Business was because he just didn't have the head for it. The man looked like he could pound you into the ground with the pad of his thumb, but he was just not any good at the finer points of the work.

"Best I can figure, you get a couple of your outdoorsy friends to come camping with you, get someone else to play the Cockadoodle." Jane opened her mouth to correct him, but when she saw Lou's exhausted look, decided it wasn't worth the energy. "And that will convince enough people that you're not him."

"Okay, solid," Jane said. "But how does this translate to money instead of just shenannigans?"

"I'm getting to that part. So what's this thing like? Like… how do the hill people give thanks or whatever?"

Lou seemed hesitant to say it out loud. "The

62

first edible thing of each harvest, but most people just leave out bread."

"No he doesn't." The wheels started turning in Reuben's head. Lou was almost certain he could see them.

"He… doesn't?"

"He takes offerings of flowers."

"He… does?"

"And the only place to get those flowers is your shop."

There was the slow tug of a smile at the corner of Lou's mouth. It was clear that he at least liked the idea in a windows sort of way. But it didn't last long before something darkened his thoughts. "Don't you think that's… a little rude?"

"We're taking people's money. It's not going to be polite." Reuben raised his eyebrows suggestively, but Lou still seemed unconvinced, until he started thinking about windows.

After a moment's silence, Jane finally spoke. "I can make a blog," she said.

"Okay, and?"

"Blogs, zines… sad little underground publications are how tourist traps get started. We can start shoving crude fliers into those newspaper crates and see how far they get."

Reuben swished this around in his mouth. "I like the way you think."

"Jane, you're not helping," Lou whispered.

"Look, Lou, I don't have the stamina to keep up all the bills in the house. This is better than nothing."

Lou made that lower-lip thinking face again, but this one was varied by the long, almost angry pause. "We'll try it your way," he said. "But if it gets even the tiniest bit out of hand, we're going back to the way it used to be."

"Agreed," he said. They shook on it, a smirk growing on Reuben's face. As soon as this thing went south, so would he.

The greenest thing on this side of the mountain.

Reuben was rudely interrupted from a dream, wherein he was being carried off in an undertow of green dollar bills, by the a loud and rhythmic tapping. He insisted on keeping his eyes closed as long as he could, determined not to be bothered by whatever it was Jane was probably doing this time. But after awhile it sounded like she was banging on the pots and pans in the kitchen and keeping his eyes closed was not going to happen.

Jane sat at the tiny dining room table with a laptop and a pocketbook full of notes. The fact that she was out in the living room and not staying in her own must have meant that she either wasn't accepting callers today or she had decided to take a day off. The already limited space of the table was covered with loose papers in no particular order.

One of them was draped poetically over the edge of the table, within arm's reach. He pulled it down to see what it was; she didn't seem to notice. *Syracor Vandalized- Local Activists Suspected,* read the headline. A grainy photo barely showed the big white building he'd passed on the way in with hastily-scrawled graffiti across the wall.

Well, that certainly had nothing to do with anything. He looked over the edge of the paper. Jane was still absorbed in whatever Twitter war she was probably wrapped up in.

"Did you sleep at all," he asked, wondering if she could even hear anything outside of her thunderous typing.

"Websites don't build themselves, buck-o."

He pried himself off the thin mattress pad, adjusting the knot in his spine from where the support bar nestled uncomfortably perpendicular to his vertebrae. She didn't notice as he peered over her shoulder at the wall of code.

"What the hell is that," he said, pointing to the block of black and white gibberish on the right side of her screen.

"HTML," she said, without so much as missing a single character.

"Why? I don't even do this computer shit and I know HTML is outdated."

"Aesthetic," she said, rolling her eyes.

He eyed the mess of papers on the table: the scribbles of notes on a legal pad, some photocopies out of books and more newspaper articles, some sad little sketches. "Where did you get all this?"

"The library."

"What kind of library is open this early?" He spied the clock in the lower right corner of her screen. It was noon. "Forget I asked that. How can they have so much information on an urban legend? No one outside of this town has ever heard about this Crackerdoodle thing."

She sighed and ceased her typing. "Dude, stop it."

"Stop what?"

"We all know you're mispronouncing it on pur-

66

pose. Like… it was funny the first couple of times, but now it's just annoying. Krikadoo. KRIK-uh-doo."

"I don't need to make jokes. The name is ridiculous enough. What kind of a name for a monster is 'Krikadoo?'"

She slid to the side of her chair, making a point to stare at him as if the very sight of him were a chore. "What'd you say you were? Pawn shop owner or something?"

He folded his arms at his chest, wondering where she was going with this. "Yeah."

"So you're telling me you never come across someone claiming that they got a legit vintage photo of Sasquatch?"

"The Krikadoo is a Sasquatch?"

"No. But the name comes from a different language that got mangled when English speakers started using the term. People from around here have roots all over Europe, the land used to be home to the Shawnee, and when people see something creeping around in the woods they're all going to call it what they think they should call it. English-speaking people come in, want to know what's going on and decide the easiest thing to call it is a Krikadoo since no one around here speaks Shawnee. Like with Sasquatch."

Reuben sat back down on the futon, finding the whole rant dull. "Wow," he said. "Pre-med, web-designer, anthropologist, and a porn star all in one."

"Cam-girl," she corrected.

"I bet you make a cunning linguist, too," he said with a grin.

She went back to typing, exhausted by the pun. "Lou's brother is an anthropologist. He visits sometimes and gets excited about cultural exchange." And then there was silence. Well, there was clacking and clicking, which wasn't exactly silence.

Reuben began flipping through one of the stacks of photocopies. She wasn't completely wrong when she mentioned Sasquatch: the photos were blurry enough that he'd mistake them for a dude in a gorilla suit. There weren't a lot of them, and none of them recent. The most recent one was from 1989 and he was pretty sure it was a bear trying to free its head from a plastic bag.

The older photos were spookier, in the way that black and white photographs were always spooky. The flash was too bright and they were trying to take a photo of something beyond the trees, but all you could see were the trees in the foreground and two glowing dots. Could have been an owl, to be honest. Or a dodge and burn darkroom trick, if they were clever hoaxters.

The older they got, the harder they were to read. Jane was right: a lot of the language choices were a mish-mash of whatever terms they could throw to-gether. His eyes were drawn to an intaglio print and a couple of stanzas.

"What the hell is this," he said, trying to read the poem. It looked like it could be English, but if someone had only learned the language phonetically and had never seen the written word in their life.

"There's a translation on the back," she said.

He flipped it over and judged her round, open handwriting and squinting at the archaic word choices.

'Beware what here lurks the wood
Something is there and well it should.
Quiet and dark like patient dusk
Old and foul like rotting husk

Happen upon him and you are blessed
Seek him out and you'll be tested
Please him and you bless your kin
Challenge him not; you cannot win

Leave for him your harvest's first
And milk or honey to quench his thirst
If you don't, tread with care
The Krikadoo always gets his share.'

"Oh, I like that," he said with a sideways grin. "The Krikadoo always gets his share.' We can do something with that. Fear makes a lasting motivator. It'll make them jump."

"I dunno," she said. "The book says that if he isn't given a proper offering, he takes the firstborn."

"So? We want them to be afraid, don't we?" His vague mob ties had taught him this, and that it was mostly effective when the person doing the motivating was a four-hundred pound chunk of muscle… which he was not. Which meant that words would have to suffice.

She sighed. "Yeah, but…" She stopped, took a deep breath. "I don't know how far you're going to take this thing."

Reuben put a hand to his chest in a mockery of offense. "I am shocked and hurt that you think that I would actually kidnap children. After all we've been through, Jane!"

"We met yesterday."

"Yesterday was a big day." What was happening on the screen suddenly took a backseat to the conversation. She ceased typing and slid to the side of her chair to face him. The length and intensity with which she stared at him made Reuben immensely uncomfortable. "What?"

"I need you to promise me that you're not doing this just so you can kidnap children," she said.

"What?"

"Don't even joke about it. Look me in the eye and tell me that I'm not helping you take kids from their homes."

He felt like he was being pushed back into the seat. "I'm just here to make money, okay?"

"There's money in human trafficking," she said. "Yes or no: are you here to fuck up some kids' lives?"

Damn, she was serious. "I promise not to kidnap kids," he said. Her stare was unwavering, as if refusing to believe it. She was studying his eyes, the twitch of his mouth, the shrug of his shoulders. Even if the idea had never crossed his mind, she made him feel guilty for even the possibility. "What? I'm not!"

She gave it another minute's contemplation before turning back to her computer. "The hair is wrong," she said cryptically.

Reuben narrowed his eyes, putting his fingers through his hair in a fit of self-awareness. "What?"

She didn't clarify, but continued her typing. He waited, expecting another weird answer, but her attention was entirely on the screen. The clacking slowed gradually, dropping like the waning of a rain storm until it stopped. She sat back in her chair, reviewing whatever it was on that screen, and making contemplative noises between her lips. Reuben leaned over to the right, trying to get a better look.

It was probably the ugliest website he had ever laid eyes on. He knew that it was brand new, she'd just coded the thing. But it looked like a relic from the 90's:

red text on a black background, links in their default royal blue. To make things worse, she kept the red and black theme throughout the articles except for photos- which looked an ugly gray against the background.

He squinted. "What… font is that?"

"Papyrus." She grinned.

"Oh god, why?"

"For authenticity."

"Its an authentic eyesore."

She hit the 'publish' button, regardless of his opinion. "Now it's a public authentic eyesore."

Jane was not a team player and Reuben didn't like that. If any of them was going to blow it, it was going to be her. He'd be keeping an eye on that web-site whenever he could. Any clues that she was the one running it were going to be the thing that brought them down.

If only he knew a damn thing about HTML.

The front door opened and Lou came sidling in. "How's the cleanup going," Jane asked.

"They said it'll be a few days before they can get the window fixed and they need the money up front, which I don't have." He shook his head. "How's the website coming?"

"Just put it up. What are you doing home so early?"

He hung his head. "Most people don't want to come into a shop that's got a big board over the front window, no matter how many signs you put up. I'm going to take a day to get rid of the pieces that I can't fridge."

"What do you do with those," Reuben asked.

"I have a place out in the woods that I use for composting. It needs to be turned soon, anyhow." At the mention of his compost heap, Jane stiffened. That repulsive, huh?

"You just… throw them back into the ground? You spend all that money on something you're just going to turn into dirt?"

Lou gave him a very blank stare. "Dirt is important."

While Reuben was busy screaming internally at the idea that money was less important than literal dirt, Lou began gathering some things from the closet. A couple large duffel bags, something plastic rustling within them.

He paused, as if unsure. He looked from Reuben to Jane "Come with me," he said to Reuben. Jane let out a small, defeated-sounding sigh. "I need someone to carry the extra bag. It's kind of a hike."

Reuben was expecting 'kind of a hike' to mean maybe walking all his shit to a dumpster, but no. He meant a literal hike out into the middle of the woods and using the trail as more of a guideline than an actual path. If Reuben had been told in the back room of his shop that he would be tromping through dirt and leaves and mud, he would have either refused to do it or at least had the forethought to buy an appropriate pair of shoes.

Instead, he was struggling to keep his funeral shoes in fair shape while sliding around on uneven ground.

But it was at least better than having Jane for company. Sure, she was fun to look at, but she seemed dedicated to irritating him at every turn. Papyrus, really?

"How does this kind of thing get started, anyhow," Reuben said, trying to keep his mind off of Jane's bra and lack thereof.

"Being a florist?"

"Being a dirt god."

Lou chuckled, kicking a walnut with his foot. He paused for awhile, trying to find the right words. To be honest, Reuben enjoyed that he spent time thinking instead of talking. When people talked just to talk, it ended up being annoying nonsense to him, which he would often have to match.

"Well, the soil around here is all kinds of messed up," he said finally. "First it was runoff from the coal mine down the way. Then when the mine closed some company was using it as a testing ground to neutralize it. That worked for a little bit, but every time the snow melts it fucks up the pH balance and you have to start over and they'll only provide soil correction for commercial farms and you have to keep doing it every year. So if you're some guy just trying to grow his own food, you're out of luck and if you just want to start a garden for the sake of having a garden, you can forget about it. And I'm not too sure that the waste runoff from the plant isn't also doing its fair share of damage, but everyone around here works for them and you can't say anything without offending someone's uncle."

The trees started thinning and Reuben could hear water, see it through the gaps in the trunks in the bright midday sun. The spot was marked by a big, red rock, and Lou didn't stop moving towards it. Reuben cringed at the implication that their destination was on the other side of the river. There were no signs of a bridge. Even if he were wearing the right kind of clothes for that, the water was disgusting. It was brown and thick and fast-moving.

"We're… going to cross that," he surmised un-easily.

Lou nodded. "I'd take off your shoes."

"I think its nice that you care about keeping my shoes clean, but they're already pretty ruined from the walk here."

Lou took a glance at Reuben's shoes as if real-izing for the first time that he was wearing wing tips. There was no possible way that he could hide the fact that he was judging him. "It's not about your shoes. Bare feet are going to have a better grip."

"Grip on what?"

Lou began untying his own boots and slinging them over his shoulder. He adjusted the weight of his bag and pulled it tighter, and without any further com-plaint- trudged on ahead towards the water.

Reuben had never really given much thought to where he drew the line for what he would and would not do for money. He was starting to compile a short list as soon as they entered the treeline, and about the time he got to the river it was quite a bit longer. Wading barefoot into heavily polluted water ought to have been the point at which he turned around and went home. All the way home: dropped off what photos he had for Needles and spend the rest of the week trying to think of interesting ways to spend his money.

So why was he rolling up the cuffs of his pants and tossing his shoes into a sack with some old soda bottles?

He was telling himself that it was because there was more money to be had if he stuck this one through. From the con, from following this dirty hippie every-where, from seeing the whole thing through until it fizzled out… there was more money in all of it if he saw it through to the end.

But truth be told, from a man who rarely told the truth… he wanted to hear the rest of the story.

So he followed in the wake of Lou's feet, regretting every second in the muddy river and yet somehow still following behind him. The dirt and rocks bowed in the middle, making a sand bar out of the deposits while still being just underneath the water enough to be massively inconvenient. If Reuben stood too long, his feet would get stuck. Lou just kept going, walking along the middle of the river like it was nothing, until the water deepened again and he was wading up to his shins. Well, on Reuben, it was his knees.

"There had better not be leeches in this," Reuben said when they came back to dry land.

"You're not gonna find leeches in running water," Lou said, shaking water and mud from his feet. He wiped his feet dry before throwing a towel at Reuben. Reuben ducked at the sudden movement of something heading towards his face and the towel landed in the water. Before he realized what had happened, he was watching the towel float downstream into rockier waters.

Concluding now that he would either have to walk barefoot or further ruin his shoes by squelching his damp feet into them, he grew angry. "You didn't have to throw it!"

"I thought you were gonna catch it."

"You should know by now that if you throw something at me, I am not going to catch it."

"Well, it wasn't a brick this time," Lou chuckled.

"Oh yeah," Reuben said, studying his shoes to see if putting wet feet into them would even matter.

"Blunt head trauma is really funny."

"When it happens to you? Yeah."

Was barefoot a thing he could do? He doubted it. The last time he went on shoeless adventures was when he was seven and stepped on a nail in his uncle's shed. Tetanus shots ruined barefootedness and unnecessary amounts of time spent outside for him for the remainder of his life.

Well, the remainder of his life until this exact moment- when he couldn't even get his socks on to act as a buffer between his feet and his insoles. Barefoot and miserable it would have to be.

"So I got the part about dirt being dirt," he said as they trudged on, him hoping that the long, thin thing he just narrowly avoided with his feet was not a snake. Lou seemed not to notice. "Where's the part where you became the local boogeyman?"

"Well, when I was little my mom used to tell me stories about the Krikadoo and a bunch of other mountain folk tales. Everyone around here believes in them a little bit, so even if you don't one-hundred percent believe in them, you learn not to cross the river because they think the Krikadoo is gonna eat them.

"And if you don't believe in them, people don't come around on this side of the hill because it used to be where folks would come to hunt and that's a good way to get shot in the leg."

"Leg?"

"I didn't say they were effective hunters."

Reuben's foot grazed across an old bullet shell. "Point taken."

"So they over-hunted or the deer moved on or one thing or another and they don't hunt as much here anymore. So all that's left is squirrels, some birds.

"But I'm not afraid of hunters and I've got no reason to be afraid of the Krikadoo, so I'm not afraid to cross the river and put the land to good use. I've been doing this for a couple years now and one day about a year ago this guy sees me from across the river. I don't think anything of it until I get back to town and someone's raving about how he saw a wildman out in the woods. Couple people whisper the name Krikadoo and it started up a couple of old traditions- like leaving out an offering. Jane gets some wicked insomnia, so she takes walks to help her wind down. She started seeing people leave out milk and honey and remembered me talking about being mistaken for the Krikadoo.

"Then I got a guilty conscience about it. I mean, if they really believe in him and if that gives them hope, then he never shows up- that's a pretty awful thing and I don't want to be the reason people give up their beliefs just because some old half-blind guy thought my dreads were roots."

"Roots? Really?"

"One of the older descriptions of the Krikadoo is that he looks like an uprooted tree."

"Country people are weird."

Lou laughed and shook his head. "They just have habits that are hard to break. And if the only way they'll learn about the pH balance of their soil is by listening to a guy in a mask, then I guess I'll be the one that wears the mask."

Reuben chewed on that for a little bit. "It sounds so much more… humble when you say it."

"What were you expecting?"

He shrugged. "I don't know… I just… if I was doing it my first inclination would be to make money off of it. Or, I dunno… it seems like it would make a fun prank if nothing else. I don't really think about other people too much."

Lou took him around a part of the hill where it looked like someone had dug a piece of it out with a giant ice cream scoop. The hill took a deep downward slope and Reuben was starting to have trouble avoiding rocks and roots with his bare feet. To no one's surprise, walking barefoot was actually more work than walking in the wrong shoes because every time he stepped on a sharp rock he had a minor heart attack that it was something like a rusty nail or a scorpion or… maybe a very small and irritated snake. He was paying so much attention to the dangers at his feet that he didn't even notice the trees becoming thinner and the light becoming brighter, greener. He was inspecting the possibility of a thorn in his big toe when he realized that Lou had slowed to a stop.

That was about when he looked up.

Lou's garden may have only taken up space within a relatively small crater- maybe slightly larger than his upsettingly small house. But he was making good use of the space regardless.

An entrance of sorts had been fashioned out of the flexible roots of an old tree, though as a gate it was quite useless. He supposed that its only real purpose was to mark where it was acceptable for humans to walk. It arched high over Reuben's head, supported by stronger, more rigid wood and lashed crudely together with some kind of twine. The only thing that might be considered a wall was a trellis running about head-height. It was intermittent and covered entirely in tenuous vines sporting small, purple flowers. He would use the word 'rustic,' to describe it.

The other word he would use to describe it was

'green.' There may have been no walls to mark it, but some of the stalks grew tall enough that they could have been walls. It was like walking into a completely different world. There were flowers that Reuben had never seen before, ones he couldn't give names to- not that it was a difficult task.

The path that was made for people to walk through was not very wide, only enough space for one person. But then, if Lou was the only person who ever came here then he supposed that there was no reason for it to be any wider. The path was not straight, preferring to meander through plants grown in semi-wild bunches rather than up and down rows like a normal person might plant them.

Reuben had accepted at face value that Lou was not a normal person.

"I thought you said you didn't have a garden," Reuben ventured.

Lou paused before answering. "Well, technically it ain't mine," he said, briefly checking on the progress of a bush of some kind. "My mom planted it and to anyone else, it belongs to the Krikadoo."

"Thought you also said you couldn't grow anything around here because of some dirt nonsense," Reuben accused, determined to catch him in at least one lie.

"There used to be a giant tree here that rotted itself out. When I was little I helped my mom spread the rotting parts around, used the whole area as a compost heap before she planted anything. This dirt," he said, punctuating it with a light kick. "Is the work of about a decade trying to make it work."

"Guess that's how you know so much about dirt, huh," Reuben surmised.

"That and some research, but most of it comes from stuff my mom showed me."

Lou took him through the path, winding past tall stalks of something pink and towards something delicately yellow before taking another turn away to bushes of something bluish. There didn't seem to be any real logic to how he'd planted them, and if Reuben didn't know better he would have guessed that they'd all grown wild.

He wished he could say that they were beautiful, but 'beautiful' was not a word that he liked to use. It was… impressive. Mostly in size and quantity, but even if parts of it did seem overgrown it was at least cared for in a way that he knew he personally would not have any patience for. It was applaudable, or would be if his hands weren't currently busy fumbling with his phone to sneak a photo.

They passed a small pond in the middle of the garden with a curious contraption jutting off the side of it. It looked like he had taken the gutter off of someone's roof and bolted it to an upright trellis. There was a grate over the top of the wide, square funnel opening. Hanging off the side of the trellis was a shallow wooden box that seemed to have no purpose.

"The hell is that about," he asked.

"It's for collecting rain water. I can't trust the water from the river, so I made a little pond."

"Looks like a mosquito breeding ground to me."

"Nah," Lou said, walking past it. "I got some minnows from a pet store. They eat the bugs before they get past the larval stage. Then I put up a bat house, so they can eat the ones that do get big enough. And then just having fresh water attracts frogs. I've got a whole little ecosystem there."

Reuben's face scrunched up when he mentioned bats, then worse at frogs. He could handle fish. Fish lived in little clear bowls on desks and never made noise or any kind of mess. Once you got into things that had legs it was a deal-breaker. And wings were out of the question.

At least he kept his pets outside, that was sure.

He took him through this garden to the opposite corner of the entrance, which was not at all impressive compared to the rest of it. It just seemed like piles of dirt in a corner, but it had Lou's interest today.

"Hand me that bag," he told Reuben. He had somehow forgotten about the sack that Lou had made him carry. It wasn't that heavy, but when he took it off it seemed like it had been weighing him down the entire time. The damn thing was full of flowers and trash, how could it be so heavy?

Lou grabbed a shovel and began digging a hole in the loose peat. The action perplexed Reuben, but about this point he was used to being perplexed. "Are you digging a grave for your flowers?"

"Well, when you put it that way," he began, turning a shovel full of dirt. "Sort of. I cut them for a purpose. They didn't get a chance to serve that purpose, so they go into the ground- decompose, start a new life as dirt and help others get a chance that they missed." Noting the confusion on Reuben's face, he simplified. "That's a poetic way of saying that it's a compost heap."

"Your life revolves around fucking dirt."

Lou seemed unfazed by what he was sure was intended as insult. "Yup."

Reuben was adamant on being wholly unhelpful by leaning on the handle of the shovel instead of dig-

81

ging. Although, Lou made it fairly clear that he didn't need help anyway and Reuben had decided that attempting to help would just be getting in the way. Ah, what a good thing that he was so good at picking up these social cues or he might have had to lift a finger.

Watching him fling dirt into the air had a slightly hypnotic effect. He could see, in a way, just how his hair might be mistaken for roots in the way that his locs hung from his head and the way they moved when he did. And he did it in such a seamless manner that yeah, he could see how someone might think he was a little otherworldly.

He started getting dizzy again and he focused on the dirt at his feet.

"Are these morels?" He moved his feet away from the little brown mushrooms to get a closer look.

Lou stopped digging for a moment to look up. "I'm surprised you know that," he said.

"Those things are like $30 a pound. You could make a mint off of these."

He went back to digging. "It takes a lot of mushrooms to make a pound. I haven't had any luck selling them, even at the street market we do on Saturdays. I usually just end up eating them."

Reuben narrowed his eyes at the idea that a man who grows and sells things for a living couldn't sell gourmet mushrooms to a bunch of yuppies. "We're going to have to work on your sales pitch."

Lou mumbled 'sales pitch' under his breath and placed his wilting lilies into the grave. He was shaking his head, but Reuben was looking around to see if there was anything else he could market better. He pointed to a daisy larger than he'd ever seen.

"How much does a thing of these go for?"

"A… bouquet?" He shrugged. "Goes about ten dollars."

"For the whole thing?"

"People usually buy them for first dates. I try to keep it in a range that broke students can afford."

"You could be charging way more." Lou shrugged it off, scooping a pile of dirt onto his flowers. "Okay, so what are these," Reuben asked, pointing to a smallish magenta flower by his ankle.

"Pinks," Lou said.

Reuben rolled his eyes. "I know what color they are," he said. "What are they called?"

Lou sighed. "Wild Pinks."

Reuben pointed accusingly at Lou. "That is a stupid name. Call them something cooler. What about these things?"

Lou wasn't looking. "What things?"

"These vine things with the purple flowers."

"Morning glories?"

"Whatever you call them. What are they worth?"

"They don't transport very well, so I don't sell them."

Reuben eyed the trellis, which was almost bursting with shades of violet and pink. "Why do you plant them if you don't intend to sell them?"

Lou paused, leaning on his shovel. He eyed the trellis, a slow smile on his face. "I like them."

"I think it's a waste of resources for something that doesn't bring in any revenue."

Lou patted dirt over his grave of lilies, sighed, and leaned the shovel against the trellis. The flowers trembled slightly at the vibration. "Haven't you ever wanted to just… build something, Reuben?"

Reuben went quiet for a solid thirty seconds. "I don't get where you're going with this."

"Just… is there anything you like to do that isn't about turning a profit?"

"Does drinking count?"

Letting out another sigh, Lou picked up the bag that used to house flowers and began checking on the rest of his garden. From his own bag, he produced a journal and began inspecting various stalks and bushes, taking notes. Occasionally, he would cut a few flowers and store them in the bag. Through all this, he seemed wholly unperturbed by the constant presence of bees and spiders.

Watching him work gave Reuben… emotions. A kind of… nostalgia for when he was young and trying to make a living. He recalled a fond smell of dust and old paper, the loud 'cha-ching' that the old cash register used to make, light streaming in through the windows at a heavy angle in mid-morning before the sun disappeared behind the neighboring building. And emptiness, significant solitude, eating mostly ramen noodles.

"I used to run a used book store," he said. Lou lifted his head, listening. "I had these dreams of having a big collection, some rare books you couldn't get anywhere else. Had an inventory and everything. One of those pricer guns that go 'ch-chunk.' But I found out pretty quick that people are more eager to get rid of their books than they are to buy them. The place filled up with shitty romance novels and even shittier suspense novels before I could do anything about it.

"No one ever bought them, not even for a dollar- they were just trying to clear up space in their basement or attic. The only way I could get rid of them is by selling them as mystery boxes online. I saw the same novel about time-traveling Vikings come through my doors five times. Not just the same title. The same book: it had a stain on the inside from what I sincerely hope was a chocolate bar.

"I stuck around for three years before I decided it wasn't worth it anymore. There are easier ways to make money off other people's junk."

Reuben wasn't really expecting much of a response. Lou was busy weeding or clipping or scribbling something very important on his note pad.

"Sounds to me like you needed to work on your sales pitch," he said, finally.

Reuben's face went tight. "Was that... what that a joke?"

"Yeah, that was a joke."

All that hard work on a personal reflection of his sad, sad life and he was laughing. "Look, all I'm saying is that I used to be just like you. This whole... living a humble life and following your dreams schtick is doomed if you keep trying to play fair. You have to put in an effort if you want to make money."

"Ah. I get it. You're having me break the law because you care."

Reuben leaned against the trellis, crushing a couple hapless morning glories in the process. Lou winced. "There are no laws against claiming to be a god."

"I think that once you start to make money off of it, they file it under 'fraud.' But... I guess you would know more about fraud than I do."

The comment was followed by a long silence in which Reuben contemplated what he was implying. Did he know? "What's that supposed to mean?"

Lou shook his head. "Nothing, it's nothing."

"That didn't sound like nothing."

Lou put down the scissors, which seemed itself a very small protest- to stop working and give him his full attention. "I don't trust you. I think you're untrustworthy."

"What an awful thing to say to someone that's trying to help you."

"I'm only doing this because honesty apparently doesn't pay the bills," he said, returning to his work.

Reuben grew a smug smile. "See, I knew you'd get it."

Lou didn't seem too amused by the implication that his only way to keep his simple life was to complicate it. He had in his bag a considerable number of flowers to be sold and he could already see a small crop of bell peppers starting to ripen and these were things that made him happy.

But he was still thinking about windows.

He continued clipping in silence, and it was in this silence that Reuben realized just how obnoxious the outdoors were. Even in the shade, the sun was bright. The more he tried to enjoy the silence, the more he realized that it wasn't silent at all. Birds, bees buzzing, the occasional croak of one of the frogs in his little pond. The more he tried to find silence between cicadas the more he realized that there was just more noise. He was fairly certain that he was getting a sunburn.

Jane was probably making the website uglier. He expected ugly animated .gifs to have been added to the front page. Maybe a header with mismatching fonts.

This gardening thing seemed like a waste of time. With all the effort spent in gardening and harvesting, he might have just gone to the store and bought it. Peppers weren't that expensive.

He spied something rolled up in the corner. He recognized it as one of those camping bed rolls. A lantern was hanging over it. "Do you actually sleep here?"

Lou followed his gaze. "Sometimes. The house doesn't have air conditioning. Mosquito bites are better than dehydration. Plus, I like it out here. It's… quiet."

Reuben disagreed, of course. He couldn't get the buzzing noise out of his head and it was just distracting. But loudest of all was Lou's scribbling on that little notepad. There was no way, from this angle, for him to see if he was making notes about him or not. That seemed like a Lou kind of thing to do- make notes about him. There was probably someone in the world compiling field notes about Reuben, waiting for enough to write a book.

Scribbling, the rustling of leaves. Stomping, careless crushing. Shit, someone was coming.

Lou stood slowly. "You're going to want to hide," he said.

"What? Why?"

Reuben heard a gunshot, Lou flinched. "Hydrangea bushes are the best spot."

"The… what?"

"The big, pink ones, over there. Now."

Reuben dashed behind the bushes and ducked just as another shot rang out. Immediately, his phone was out and he was using it as a periscope. Two men came trotting towards the garden, Lou went to meet them.

He couldn't see Lou's expression since it was mostly the back of his head, but he didn't seem happy. It was as though every kind of movement stopped, even the bees seemed to cease their buzzing in favor of waiting for him to speak.

"Don't ever point a gun at me again," he said. If boulders could speak, they would sound like Lou right now.

"Oh, my bad," said a very fat ginger. They were dressed in camouflage and each had a hunting rifle. It didn't take a genius to realize what they were doing here. "I thought you were a bear."

"There are no bears here. No deer. They've all been scared off and moved south."

"Hey, you know Tim- I thought we told this guy to skeedaddle," said a rail-thin man with a ponytail poking out the back of his camo baseball hat.

"You know, I believe we did. We did, didn't we?"

"You don't own this land," Lou said. Reuben could see his hands begin to form into fists.

"You don't either, buddy."

"Then I guess we are both here illegally. The only thing left to do is to stay out of each other's way unless we want to get the Cops involved. And since there are more restrictions on hunting than there are growing tomatoes, I can take a guess who they'll want to investigate first."

Tim and his reedy friend chewed on this for a moment. The bees began their buzzing again, having lost interest in what was happening and become preoccupied with more important things than whatever drama was happening between humans.

Don't get mad, Lou's posture seemed to say. *Don't get mad, don't get mad.*

"Don't think this ain't over," the ginger said as they turned. Reuben wanted to correct his grammar, pointing out the double negative, but decided in favor of hiding in this bush.

They disappeared behind a bend in the hill and Lou seemed to deflate an inch or two. Reuben's head popped out of the hydrangea bush, little florets getting stuck in his hair and one clinging to his goatee. "What was that all about?"

"Pretty much what it looks like," Lou said, gathering up what he'd harvested for the day. He filled a couple bottles of water from the pond, scattering a handful of frogs in every direction- except for one stubborn bull frog that seemed set on staying right where he was. He bound his cuttings together and set them in the water, wrapping a bag loosely over the top of each of them. "They're just some jerks that think they own this place because they have a couple of guns."

"What if one of them shot you?"

"The only way they would have killed me is if they were aiming for my feet and missed. I told you- they're a bad shot." He had about three of his cuttings encapsulated in their little miniature greenhouses, with another ten to go.

"Okay, so what if one of them aimed for the head and shot you in the foot?"

Lou thought about that for a moment, tilting his head skyward and calculating the likelihood."That would suck." He shrugged and went back to working.

"That's it? You'd just take it?"

"Pretty much."

"You would take… a bullet to the foot."

"What? It's a foot."

"Yeah, but its your foot."

"I'd probably call Jane and have her call 911. She's better at coming up with a lie than I am."

"So you'll have someone else lie for you, but you don't like lying yourself," Reuben said, feeling pretty proud of himself for that deduction. Lou started gathering up the few peppers and strawberries that had grown, the cuttings of herbs which looked like they could live on forever if he let them, and putting them in a different bag. "Its because you're not good at it, I bet."

Lou hoisted both bags up onto his shoulders. "To get good at something, you have to practice at it. I'm proud of myself for not being good at lying."

"How is pretending to be a god not lying?"

"That's different. Its acting."

"Which is not lying… how?"

"I didn't say that it wasn't. But I wasn't making money off of it and now I am and that puts it on another level."

"Well, if you want out, you just have to say so. I can wear the scary mask and tell people what to do. And Jane seems on board with everything so I guess we don't really need you." Lou began tromping off towards the exit, or rather the ancient root that signified the exit. When he didn't respond, Reuben became anxious. He was just going to keep walking and he couldn't make a comment like that and then trail behind him like a lost puppy. "Okay fine, maybe we need you. But you need to be okay with lying."

Take one down, pass it around.

   They returned to the house muddy and still talking. Well, Reuben was talking. Lou was… making a point of not talking. It would have been rude to interrupt, and since the man didn't have much in the art of a dramatic pause there was no space to speak. But then… there wasn't much to really say. Reuben was still trying to convince him that he was needed. Or… not needed. It really wasn't all that clear. He seemed to be waffling between threatening to take this on his own and trying to persuade him that he would really be the major beneficiary.

   Of course, Lou never officially voiced any interest in leaving. But his refusal to take part in the conversation had Reuben on edge. So when they finally arrived at the slightly tilted front door, it was announced with Reuben loudly disintegrating into begging.

   "I'm just saying… it doesn't make sense for us to be doing this without you. I mean, I'll still find a way to turn a profit off of it, but it's going to be easier if you're part of it. So please reconsider." Perhaps not begging. Almost begging. Reuben had mastered the art of almost begging.

   There was finally a pause in Reuben's words and Lou had a moment to respond.

   "Okay," he said.

   And for once, Reuben was speechless- even if it

didn't last very long. "That's it? Just 'okay,' and you're back in?"

"I... never said that I was out. You just... kind of assumed."

"Then why didn't you say anything?"

Lou poised himself at eye-level, which meant bending just a little at the waist. "When you're worried," he said. "You get this little crease in the spot between your eyebrows." He hovered a finger directly over where that very crease was starting to form.

Reuben self-consciously covered his forehead with his hand. "So?"

He stood back up. "I wanna see if I can make a permanent dent in it."

"So you're still in."

"Yeah, sure."

Reuben took his hand down. "Then there's nothing to worry about."

Lou studied his face, as if trying to decide whether the solid hour of worrying had made a difference before shrugging it off.

The kitchen was stacked high with papers and Jane was sleeping at the table with her laptop still open. She was done setting up the site and it looked like she was finding ways to promote it on social media. A Facebook page had been made, and she was just about to design an advertisement before she crashed.

Reuben pondered the ethical implications of what he should do with an unattended Facebook account for an entire three seconds before doing what he planned to do what he wanted anyway. Carefully reaching over her, he began typing.

"I don't think," Lou started, but he was immediately shushed.

"Dude, do you want to wake her up?"

And knowing that it took a considerable amount of exhaustion to get Jane to actually fall asleep, Lou conceded that it was best if she wasn't woken. But he simmered quietly while he watched Reuben fill in the blanks, scroll over a few tabs, and approve the ad in Jane's name.

"What did you just do?"

"I wrote a better ad than she was gonna give us."

Deciding it was best not to pry into the business of the business-people, Lou began carefully emptying the contents of the sack into the fridge. It was no surprise that there wasn't much actual food in that fridge. Most of it was either vegetables or pickled and jarred, many of which he recognized from the market stalls. He had taken a peek at the cabinets earlier: dried and boxed.

They'd been feeding him soup. It seemed like all they ate was soup. Lou might be making it go further with some vegetables, but it was canned soup- the kind that came out of the can in a solid form and accompanied by a 'schloop' sound. It was disgusting, but it was better than ramen noodles.

Reuben took a look at the piles of paper on the kitchen table. There were more of them now, and they didn't look like research materials. He pulled one of them off the stack.

The same drawing of a shadowy figure that served as a banner on the website overlooked a half-sheet with the word 'KRIKADOO' scrawled beneath it. The second 'K' was purposely written backwards. He flipped it over, expecting there to be more, but it was blank. The rest of the stack were identical.

"What the hell is this?"

The exclamation was just loud enough for Jane to wake up. She bolt upright in her chair, knocking it back onto two legs for a fraction of a second. She babbled something incoherent before staring blankly at her screen for twenty seconds.

"Um… what?"

"Muenster cheese," Lou said.

"What," they chorused. Reuben looked at him, not entirely sure what just happened or… why it happened. Jane was focusing heavily on the empty space in front of her.

"She said… 'muenster cheese.'"

"That shit is awesome," she said.

"Damn," Lou said. "Now I want a grilled cheese."

"Okay, better question," Reuben said, pointing to the half-sheets. "What the hell is this?"

"It's a… flier," she said, bewildered by the question. "What about it?"

"There's no information on it. How are they supposed to know what it is?"

She already looked exhausted by the conversation. "Because half the town already knows what it is. The point is to get people searching for it. They search it, they land on the site. All goes as planned, people start getting curious or paranoid and start looking for ways to participate. Annnnd we make money off of it." She rolled her hand at the joint of her wrist. "Somehow."

Reuben found the logic in it, but he wasn't convinced. Or rather, he wasn't comfortable with the idea that she seemed to have a handle on all of it. "This just doesn't sound like good marketing to me."

"If it doesn't work, we'll try another approach and see what sticks."

"I'm guessing you were a business major for a semester, too."

"I took an online class."

Reuben made a mental note to find at least one thing in this damn world that Jane didn't know the basics of. But then, for it to be a real victory, he would have to know how to do it in her place- and that meant effort.

She swung herself around in her chair and lifted the stack up off the table, handing one third of it to Reuben. "This one's for you," she said. She portioned one for herself and tapped Lou on the shoulder. He spun around while taking a bite out of a bell pepper.

"Are you just… eating a raw pepper," Reuben asked. "That thing was growing out of the ground an hour ago.

"They're good," Lou said with a shrug, taking the stack of papers. "I take it we're going to be handing these out?"

"Don't hand them to anyone," Reuben insisted. "Then they'll know who's doing it."

"Which is why we're going to be posting them on phone poles and stuff," Jane said.

Reuben continued to simmer. If Jane was just going to do whatever she wanted in this scam, then it was going to be a problem. They all needed to be on the same page if they were going to pull this off, and she was making things happen much more quickly than he was expecting.

"I'm going to do my usual route. You two wanna do downtown?"

"Sure," Lou offered before Reuben could

protest. Of course… he had no real reason to protest other than for the sake of protesting, which was a good enough reason for him.

"Cool. Its getting dark out. As long as we're sneaky about it, I don't think anyone will really notice us. See you guys later." She took her stack and escaped out the door before anything else could be said.

Lou let out a heavy sigh, watching the door close behind her.

"I take it she does this a lot, huh," Reuben commented.

"Go off on her own after getting less than an hour of sleep? Yes." He sighed again. "I can't get too worried. She always comes back."

"What if she tells someone?"

"About what?"

"About… this?" He indicated the stack of fliers in his hand.

"Well, then I guess we're done and we go back to what we were doing." He shrugged, heading for the door.

"Well don't look too upset about it," he said, following Lou out to his car.

There was a remarkable difference between night in the city and night out here in this little town. As soon as the sun went down, it was quiet here. Of course, nothing was truly quiet and the more he listened for silence the more he realized that he would never find it. But the noises were… less noisy. They were things like crickets and the occasional passing car, maybe a plane overhead. Even the street lamps seemed less aggressive- they gave a gentle warm glow instead of orange. The air was thick with the sharp scent of decorative pansies that marked every twenty feet of the sidewalk.

He didn't like it. It all seemed suspicious.

"If you want to take the west side of town, I'll take the east side," Lou said, getting out of the car.

"Which way is west?" Lou pointed to the faint glow of the sun on the horizon, which left the sky a slightly blushing color. Even the fucking sky was suspiciously quaint. "Oh. That west. How long do you think it'll take?"

"A couple hours," he said, waffling a little as he judged the size of downtown. Reuben thought that was a generous approximation. This place was tiny and there were only so many light posts.

His eyes were drifting over to his station wagon, which was still sitting in the parking lot across the street. He wasn't about to go another day in the same set of clothes, especially after that trek through the river. His feet were itchy already.

"I guess I'll see you in a couple hours," he said. Lou smiled. Reuben didn't get why.

As soon as Lou had turned a corner and was out of sight, Reuben threw his stack straight into a waste bin and began heading towards his car.

Within the past three days, it had collected even more pamphlets from the homeless shelter, a flier about some kind of concert going on in the next town over, and a bright orange sticker indicating that the car was abandoned. He pulled all of it off, scraping the orange sticker off and throwing all of it, including Waving Jesus, into the garbage.

He had a wandering thought: he had his car now. He didn't need to rely on Lou to cart him around. And even though he didn't really know his way around town, he did know the road to get out.

He could leave.

He was certain that Lou was the wrong guy. He was too honest and all he wanted was to work in his shop and play in the dirt.

And this scam he was running probably would be fine without him. It probably wouldn't make the kind of money he was hoping. Jane would probably take his share of the profits even if it did. In the long run, it didn't matter if he left right now.

"Weller." His hand was on the door handle when he heard a voice that he didn't associate with small towns or potted pansies at all. Reuben spun around and there was Needles, looking just about as seedy as ever. He was not accompanied by The Shark, which he personally found curious. Reuben could only assume that there was nothing at all threatening about this town and there would never be a need for protection.

"Needles… I was just about to call you."

"It's been three days. We were starting to worry."

Now, that was an outright lie and Reuben knew it. Needles didn't worry, at least not about people.

"Hey, no need to worry about me, man. I've got this whole thing worked out."

"It's not you I'm worried about," Needles said. "I'm starting to bleed cash to pay you for what looks like fucking around."

"Fucking around?" Reuben took on an indignant look. "I am getting close to him, like you said."

"Did I see you two come into town together? Did you move in with him?"

Reuben was hesitant to answer. "...technically?"

"This had better get me results, Weller. You know what happens when people try to play us."

Needles pivoted and began walking off. The wheels in Reuben's head began turning again and it took two or three clicks before he finally realized why Needles was so desperate to get Lou in trouble.

"I get it," Reuben surmised. "Moretti didn't hire me, you did." Needles stopped in mid-step. "Lou wouldn't hurt a fly. I'm going to go out on a limb here and say you're the one that slipped up. You're the one that gets in trouble if Lou runs his mouth- Moretti could care less."

Needles turned to face him. "Can't keep a secret around you, can I?"

"You can buy my silence." Reuben said. It was unclear whether he was joking or serious. For all anyone would be able to tell, Reuben didn't know either.

Needles twitched a smile, not so much because he found him amusing but because baring his pointed teeth was a natural reaction to that kind of a comment. "I'll pay you when I get results."

"Then you don't need to worry about anything," Reuben said smugly to Needle's back. To be honest, he was a little flattered: he came all this way just to tell him off. That was easily a two-hour drive he could have done without and could have been done with a phone call. Maybe he did care.

Well, that ate up all of twenty minutes and he still had an entire half of town to not plaster with fliers. He had his change of clothes and though the thought of leaving this circus was tempting… if he flaked just after having that talk with Needles, he wasn't going to get paid for sure. He could probably kiss any future paying jobs good-bye as well.

So now it was going to be about focus, and that meant that there would come a point where he might have to sabotage his own con to get the photos he needed. Damn, well… at least he was going to make this interesting.

Ah, but for it to be anything, the con had to be a success. He was planning on running off with the money in the end anyway, but now… he had to time it just right. He had to have just a little bit of success and then tear it all to shreds.

Well… failing was something he knew how to do. Arguably, it might be the only thing he was actually good at.

His feet took him up Haute St, going no direction in particular. By habit, he only became aware of his surroundings when he heard the clinking of glasses. Reuben was starting to wonder why, exactly, Lou would only go into the one bar on the other side of town. This one didn't look too different from the one he'd taken him to, it even had the umbrellas out in the front.

The interior had a concerning lack of mounted tricycle, and Reuben decided that he liked this place already. The place was not in any way fancy: wood countertop and some kind of wrestling match on the television in the corner. The patrons were all wearing billed hats.

It was a bar. It was just… a bar. Not a bar and… just a bar.

Thank god. Finally this place was starting to look like it had culture.

He was halfway through his first gin and tonic when two more people came in. He recognized them immediately as the two guys that came to Lou's garden, and sure enough that was a white truck parked out front. And of course, there were other white trucks in this town, but if anyone seemed like they might want to break a window, these two were definitely candidates-especially with their notable bad aim.

They took a seat at the bar and he was extremely aware of the pain along the side of his head, and the way that the stitches caused a ridge. Jane had not done a good job. It was better than nothing, but that thing wasn't going to go away even if it healed well. Big red scar right by his temple all because some yokels thought it would be great to throw a rock into someone's window.

He worked himself up into a rage, but now he didn't know what to do with it. He began clenching and unclenching his jaw, sliding the cardboard coaster back and forth on the high-gloss table with his fingers. His anger just sat there, burning in his gut while he tried to shoot lasers out of his eyes.

It was interrupted by the brief buzzing of his phone. Who the hell would be calling him when he was clearly plotting revenge?

It was a text from an unlisted number. *What r u doing?*

Reuben looked around the bar, but everyone was either chatting with their friends or watching the match. A movement in the window caught his eye. Lou was standing outside, just around the corner of the brick storefront. He could vaguely see the outline of his knitted hat.

Having a drink. Your hunting buddies are here.

He watched Lou's shadow roll towards the window for a quick moment before hiding back behind that brick wall. *Now u know why i don't come here.*

For someone who put a lot of energy into hiding his double life as a local deity, Lou was not very gutsy. Reuben was fidgeting with the coaster again. The hunters still had their backs to him. He had the perfect chance to do something about his anger right now.

He loosened his jaw and rose from his seat.

There was another buzz from his phone that was undoubtedly Lou asking him what he was doing. He took a look at the screen they were both watching. Boxing, not wrestling. That was harder. There was less of a script.

He took a seat at the bar, a comfortable one stool away from the two of them. "Twenty bucks says the guy in the green shorts wins this round."

Two pairs of eyes on him, Tim made an extra effort to lean forward and squint.

"You're crazy, dude," said Tim. He pointed to the opponent in blue. "That's Doughan. He's unbeatable. And Wester is a rookie compared to him."

"Twenty bucks," Reuben said.

"If you're right, you get twenty. But if he loses the first round, you owe each of us twenty. So that's forty."

"That is not fair."

"My mistake, buddy. I thought that given the circumstances, you were probably a crazy person."

"You know what? Deal. He wins this round, forty."

Tim gave his buddy a nod. "Watch this," he said. The bell rang and the two were dancing around the ring and taking jabs at each other. Wester in the Green Shorts was doing more dodging than he was punching and Doughan was just giving him throw after throw. He slowed and became more calculated, conserving his moves to make them count. And it was one lucky punch from Wester that started that wave back at him. Doughan couldn't keep up. Smacked him straight into the corner. Doughan was down.

Tim and his cohort turned to Reuben in disbelief before they started digging through their wallets.

But Reuben wasn't satisfied. "Fifty says the rookie wins the match."

"You're a nut," Tim proclaimed. "That round was a fluke."

"If I'm wrong, I owe fifty each."

Tim turned back to the TV. Wester's legs were shaking and he was wound up from the victory of the last round. Doughan, on the other hand, had a stone face of determination.

"You're on, stranger."

The bell rang for the third round and Wester took the first swing, blocked. Another swing, dodged. Wester as bouncing around the ring, trying to find his angle. Doughan met him at every single one. But the moment that the rookie started losing his steam Doughan was back with enough force to knock him back again. Wester started wobbling, Doughan took advantage of this and Wester was on the ground no time.

Reuben hid his grin when the other two turned back to him. "Pay up, dude."

Reuben conceded and handed him a couple of fifties. "You got me. I'll get it next time."

"Next time don't bet on the loser." Tim and his friend shared a high-five.

Lou was surprised to see Reuben exit the bar with a smile on his face.

"That was painful to watch," Lou said, shaking his head. "What the hell were you doing?"

"I was just paying them back for the number they did on my skull," he said, pointing to the wound on his forehead.

"Paying them back? Reuben, you lost."

"Did I," he asked wistfully.

Unsure how else to respond to a comment like that, Lou rolled his eyes. "Yes. You did. You lost one hundred dollars."

"And by the time they realize that those fifties were fakes, they'll have forgotten where they got them."

Lou was silent, which wasn't uncommon in and of itself but for the intensity in which it was delivered. He pulled Reuben off into an alley. "Why do you have counterfeit bills?"

"Are you telling me that you… don't?"

Lou's eyebrows turned downward. You never realize how big a man's eyebrows are until they're turned downwards. "No."

"You've been running that business how long and you've never come across a single counterfeit bill?"

"I don't keep them. I give them to the bank to dispose of."

"Why would you do that?"

"Because it's what you're supposed to do."

This was a nice alley. There wasn't any trash on the ground or broken glass. Reuben got the sense that people didn't sleep here. Even their alleyways were nice. What the hell was that about?

"You should know by now that I don't do what I'm supposed to do."

"I've only known you for three days."

"Really? Feels like longer."

"If they find out that you've been doing this, they can put you in jail."

"Counterfeits go into circulation all the time and people don't realize it. They'd have to prove that I knew what it was."

"But you did know what it was."

Reuben paused. "Are you seriously going to tell the cops? Because that really throws a wrench in this plan to make you rich."

Lou stopped talking. The conversation's end was marked with a heavy sigh. "I just… a lot of this scares me and I don't want to get involved in anything that's going to get us in trouble."

They started moving back out onto the sidewalk. "And as long as you don't tell anyone," Reuben said. "We won't get in any trouble."

Lou followed. "Where are you going?"

"Back to my car? I'm done with the fliers."

"You've been drinking."

He threw his hands to his side, keys in hand. "I had one drink."

Lou snatched the keys from him. It surprised him how fast Lou could be. He always walked with a steady gait, he didn't seem the type to take things abruptly. "Jane says it takes ten days for your brain to heal. I'm not letting you drive."

"Jane learned to stitch up a wound from You-tube." Reuben reached to take his keys, but Lou pulled them away. He dangled them above him, jingling them tauntingly. "You are acting childish."

"I figured I would level the playing field, since you're not acting at all." Reuben attempted to take them while he was talking, but it was true- he was starting to feel dizzy again and missed. "I will take you into town again tomorrow. You can get your car then when you're sober."

He was starting to think that Lou liked having him where he could see him. Well, that wasn't going to

105

be a problem, because this closet control freak was going to be right next to him until he got what he needed.

A moment of silence for Reuben's traumatic childhood.

      Reuben did not like it when other people drove, and predictably it was a trust issue.

      Once, when he was approximately seven years old, his mother had gone into the grocery store and left him in the car because it was 'only going to be a minute.' Seven-year-old Reuben Weller thought that he'd be fine until the car started rolling backwards. Inconveniently, a construction crew was digging a ditch directly behind the car as it slowly headed away from the parking lot and down the decline. Seven-year-old Reuben Weller panicked as he tried to figure out which pedal was the one that made the car stop and which was the one that made the car go. The minivan stopped moving when it landed in the ditch and it didn't matter anymore, but he remembered strange men crowding around the windows to get him out. And crying. Lots of crying.

      That's the sort of thing that sticks with you: he couldn't trust someone to not leave the car in neutral instead of park. Seven was a big year for Reuben. It was the year that he developed a fear of taxi drivers and learned never to take his shoes off outside.

      He also didn't trust anyone not to drive him off a bridge and Lou's car was the kind that had the child safety lock function, not that he'd use it. Still, he liked the illusion of control when he was driving.

Which was why he was up curiously early the next morning to retrieve his driving privileges. As soon as Lou was parked behind the building, he was out the door and heading towards the parking lot across the street.

"You're not even gonna help me bring the new stuff in?"

Reuben pivoted. Lou was at the trunk of the car, balancing a couple vases of wildflowers in his arms. There were about four more still in the trunk. Well, fine. If he was going to make that face at him.

Lou juggled with the vases while trying to unlock the back door. The back of the building looked… less pleasant than the front of it. Not dirty or unsafe, but certainly not welcoming like the facade. He found a strange comfort in this: at least not everything in downtown was picturesque. It said something to him in a symbolic sort of way. Places where people live are a reflection of the people that live in them. The tiny bit of graffiti on the wall made him feel a little more at home. Thank you, whoever you are. Your confession of 'Felicia is a ho' is an artistic contribution to this community.

The back of the store was not at all interesting. Along a narrow hallway was a bank of refrigeration units full of flowers. He recognized some of the same flowers from the front of the store. Lou must have put them back here to keep them fresh while they were getting the window fixed. Which, judging by the lack of light coming in through the front room, was not going very well. He'd traded the tarp for a piece of board, which was at least keeping the wind out, but damn it was dark in there.

Reuben was used to dark. Reuben liked dark. Lou, on the other hand…

108

Lou existed for sunlight, and the absence of it in his shop seemed to make everything want to wither and wilt.

The glass had been cleaned up and he'd moved the displays away from the broken window where they could get what light they could. He'd been making use of the space he had, but the place still looked empty. He might even venture to say that it looked… sad. He didn't like putting emotions to things that couldn't feel, but right now… it was very sad.

"What do you do all day if you're not getting customers," Reuben asked.

"Wow, rude," Lou said while putting a vase of daisies on a shelf. "I clean, mostly. Put some arrangements together. I have a couple ideas that normally I wouldn't have time to do but...well… blessing in disguise, I guess. Otherwise… I guess I do a lot of waiting." He adjusted some of the flowers in the fridge, trying to see if they were wilting or if he was just not happy with anything. "But I can't say that I've ever been terribly busy. Maybe one or two customers a day during the week."

Those were scary numbers for Reuben. "Seriously? How do you even pay rent on the place?"

"I don't."

"...what?"

"I kind of inherited this place from my mom. It used to be a boutique up until the 50s, then this whole row was just a bunch of abandoned storefronts. She bought it for $100 in the 70's, or at least that's what she told me- pretty sure it was more than that, but she liked to exaggerate. Started her business, had kids, passed the trade on. So I own the place and just gotta pay utilities, which I cut down a little bit with a solar panel on the roof."

"If I were you," Reuben offered. "I would ditch the shitty house and roommate situation and sleep in the store."

Lou chuckled. "I'd rather not. Its nice to be able to go home and have an escape from work. Besides, I like having Jane around."

"I'd be willing to believe that if I hadn't just forded a river so you could do work off the clock."

"That's different. I like gardening. I don't like finding busy work to do while I wait for customers to walk in." He chose an armful of tissue paper from a box in the back, a wide array of different colors all cut in perfect little squares. "But it's a necessary thing, I guess. If you want to make money, you have to deal with people, who are harder to deal with than flowers."

Someone had been reading one too many new age books, Reuben surmised. This was further evidenced by something that caught his eye in the corner. It was a little flickering glow of what looked like an electric candle.

It was a little end table with a display not unlike the one that Lou had in his bedroom. There was only one wooden figure, though: a bird. If Reuben had to guess, he might have said it was a sparrow or a swallow or a finch. But that really wasn't something he knew enough about. It was a bird. Set up on a little pedestal that he was pretty sure was a spice rack at some point in its life was a row of photos.

The photos were old. A couple of them were in black and white, but most of them were recent enough that they were in color. Although, they did carry the brownish tinge that came from not knowing how to stage lighting or correct white balance. He could barely see the woman in the photo- her dark skin almost blended completely with the faded background. It was almost as if her smile and her eyes were emerging from the darkness.

She looked familiar, in a way that he couldn't quite place.

He got a strange mix of feeling from this little shrine. It was happy and sad at the same time. He didn't like this kind of complexity- if he couldn't boil it down to one or the other, then it wasn't worth his contemplation.

Lou's places had emotions and that confused him.

"You need anything else from me," Reuben asked, turning away before Lou could catch him spying.

Lou looked back at his fridge full of flowers. "No, I think you're good to go."

And Reuben was out the door just moments after he heard Lou mumble 'rude.'

He was about halfway towards the lot when he heard a door slam behind him. He knew it was a cop car before he turned around- cop cars always sounded heavy to him. It was the same cop that had come when he called about the drums, Officer Mike, and he had a piece of paper in his hand. Soon after Lou switched the sign on the door to 'open,' the cop stormed in.

Oh, he had to see this.

Reuben kept himself hidden from behind the wooden plank where the window used to be. The sounds were muffled by it, but not nearly as much as they would have been if it were glass.

"What is this," said the cop. He held up the paper. It was, beyond any shadow of a doubt, one of the fliers that they'd been putting up the night before.

111

"It's nice to see you, too, Mike," Lou said. And out went Reuben's phone, snapping some photos just in case he got something useful. Carefully staging things wasn't working. Now it was about getting as many shots in as he could and hoping for the best.

"Lou, I told you- no more weird shit."

"That ain't mine, though," he said. Reuben sneaked a peek over the edge of the wood board. Lou had a very sincere look on his face, and it occurred to Reuben that he wasn't technically lying. They weren't his, they were Jane's. The man knew how to be dishonest when it suited him and he found that an endearing quality.

The cop let go of the tense sort of face that cops have, allowed it to soften. "Look, I know what you're doing."

"...sweeping?"

"Put down the broom." The cop sighed and there was a light tap as he set the broom against the wall. "I know you want to stay close to your mother, but this is now how you do it. Rhonda was sick. All that weirdness she was into was a symptom of that. You have to let it go." Lou responded with his signature silence, which felt like it went on for a good minute. "I'm trying to look out for you here."

"Don't," Lou commanded. "You're talking about her like she's dead. If you're not gonna try to understand me, then you're not gonna be able to help. I already told you that ain't mine, so you can stop worrying."

The two of them were trapped in a tense silence, broken only when a staticy voice tried to contact him over the radio. He mumbled something about being right there and Reuben took that as his cue to dart out of sight.

The cop went straight to his car and drove off.

Reuben made a point of looking busy as he walked to his car, but he didn't get far before he felt a buzzing in his back pocket. He looked back across the street to see Lou holding his phone in his hands, staring at him through one of the unbroken windows.

He hated this kind of communication. It was so traceable, even if he ended up deleting his messages there was always the chance that someone might be watching his phone. You never knew what the government was up to, even for a small-time crook like him.

I'm having second thoughts, Lou's text read.
You were already having second thoughts.

Through the window, and even from this distance across the street, the flat and unamused expression on Lou's face was visible. It was probably visible from space, if anyone were curious enough to look.

I'm having third thoughts. Reuben rolled his eyes. When they rolled back, Lou was typing again, and the little ellipsis on Reuben's phone was doing its little dance. *I think someone's going to find out.*

Lou really was hopeless. By the end of this, he was going to teach the man how to have a backup plan.

So you have to misdirect them.

Lou's vague shadow sagged. *I don't know how to do that.*

He was going to have to teach this man everything. *Leave it to me, I'll come up with something.*

Reuben spent the better part of the morning getting to know the town a little better, just in case he needed to ditch the do-gooder in a hurry. The place was so clean, so well-lit… he hated it. They emptied the trash bins here, who does that? But the further he got away from the highway, the closer the buildings were tucked together. The alley ways were smaller, easier to hide in, and took unexpected turns. They were more prone to graffiti and decay.

He liked that. He liked those little hiding spots where people only went to cause mischief. At least not everyone in these hills was out to make him look bad.

He drove around until things started looking familiar, buildings stopped looking quaint and started looking like people actually lived there. The line of trees that marked the edge of the liveable land and the little, white brick building that sat on its edge was right where he'd left it a few hours ago.

There was a motel closer to the highway, he kept reminding himself. And he could always go back to sleeping in the car because honestly that back seat was almost home to him. He could just as easily move his car somewhere else and avoid getting his windshield another coat of pamphlets.

But this was free and wasn't going to get him any loitering tickets.

He was expecting the door to be locked, but when he tried to jiggle the knob it just swung open without even trying. The place was in a state of disarray, but that was nothing new. The place was always in a state of disarray.

"Hey, anyone home," Reuben called. There was no answer. He ventured through the hall, wondering if they just hadn't heard him. There was still evidence of Jane working on the website- papers everywhere and her laptop sitting open, but she wasn't there.Jane's door was open a crack, but he was pretty sure she wasn't there or he would have heard… noises.

Well, it was her damn fault for leaving both the front door and her bedroom door open, and he'd already pretty much figured Lou out. It was time to see what Jane of All Trades lived like.

The first thing he noticed was the camera setup in front of the bed, along with a 24 inch screen. If it wouldn't be damning evidence, he would have taken a look through to see what video went with the sound track.

The only thing in the room that he would have considered 'clean' was the bed. Pillows were arranged neatly and artistically, sheets were clean, blankets were folded.

And then there was the collection of dildoes, displayed proudly on the shelf behind the bed. There were… so many. He didn't want to know how many of them there were, thirty-six, because just the sight of that many, arranged by color and size and evenly spaced, made him just a tad uncomfortable. Particularly the ones on the bottom shelf, which were larger than his forearm and lovingly modeled with realistic veins. He was also trying not to think how many of them were in that trunk by the foot of the bed.

And now he was focusing on literally anything else in the room, which was a complete mess. The bed was a stage, he'd figured, and probably all you could see from the camera anyway. It was like night and day, really. She kept dishes piled up in the corners, clothes in odd places around the floor. Trash. He could see that at some point she'd made an effort to clean, but she'd gotten as far as putting trash in a plastic bag before giving up.

That pretty much summed up Jane's space: a mess and thirty-six dildoes. He wasn't sure what he expected, to be honest.

Along the wall was a cork board arranged with news clippings. She didn't… seem the type of person to have a crazy wall, but it didn't seem like she was connecting any conspiracy theories so much as she was collecting scraps. There was a picture of a little blonde girl. *Syracor Children Still Missing,* read one. *Juniper Lawson Testifies Against Local Cult.*

He was about to skim the rest of them when he heard footsteps coming towards the house. Not the heavy feet that Lou walked with, but something lighter and quicker. Jane was coming and he needed to get out of there.

He'd made it to the kitchen by the time the door opened, and decided that the most logical thing to do was open the fridge. The second she saw him, she put a hand on her hip- already fed up with him for the day.

"Do you just raid everyone's fridge the minute you become friends with them," she asked.

"You left your door unlocked, I just assumed the rest of the place was fair game."

He saw her close the gap in the door to her bedroom. "The only other two people living on this block are a woman I've never seen leave her house and an immigrant couple from Romania. The only person up here that I don't trust is… well, I guess that would be you."

"I am totally trustworthy," Reuben said, shoving a piece of cheese into his mouth for authenticity. He had to concur: muenster was the superior cheese. She didn't have a comeback, just a very flat expression.

"Why are you still here?"

"You're expecting me to be gone? We've got a con to run."

Hip. "Usually the guy that causes the trouble

116

isn't around to take the blame when the going gets tough."

"It hasn't gotten tough yet," he said. "No thanks to you, I might add."

"Me? What about you? I'm the one doing all the work here. The only thing I've seen you actually do is eat out of our fridge."

"Your little fliers are not nearly as anonymous as you think they are. Lou got in trouble today because some cop found it and thought it was his. So thanks to your little marketing ploy, we have to throw them off the scent."

There was that flat expression again. It was like she didn't even have emotions. Or maybe it was that she didn't like having them. "People around here get jumpy about the pagan stuff, Reuben."

"People are always jumpy about it. There's a lady that hands out Chick Tracts on my corner and I can't legally tell her to leave."

She sighed, flipping through a few of the articles she'd compiled on the dining room table. "This town has a history of it. Couple decades ago, there was a lot of interest in folk cultures and this place got to be known for… things." Reuben rolled his wrist at her, imploring her to elaborate. "Cults, Reuben. We had a cult."

He furrowed an eyebrow. "What? That has to be an exaggeration." He wasn't about to take at face-value what the newspapers said. The newspapers said a lot of things; that's how you sell newspapers.

She sighed. "It's not. People started getting heavy into the local folktales right around the same time they built the plant down the hill. People would meet out in the woods and do rituals and shit."

117

See, this is the kind of thing that happens in little towns that no one ever visits. They all start to get a screw loose from seeing the same people every day. And sure, it was weird and creepy but as far as he was concerned that wasn't any reason for the cops to be so damn nervous. But Jane was looking a little nervous herself. Not in the normal person kind of way because that was not how she did things like emotions. But she was looking off in directions that weren't him, and that was a tell enough for Reuben.

"Something bad happened, didn't it?"

"Stuff… started happening," she said. "People don't like to talk about it much and I was like eight years old so I only know what I heard."

She was trying to get him to drop it, but that wasn't going over well for Reuben. Now she had him hooked on the story and he needed to hear the rest of it. Of course, it was because he was worried about what would happen if he went too far and not at all because he was engrossed in all the weird things that country people do. Of course, it was all about concern. "So are you gonna tell me what it was?"

"People went missing," she said.

"Just… missing?"

She nodded. "Five kids, Youngest was 5, oldest was 12. They were the kids of some people who worked at the plant. They were out playing. Their parents turned their heads for a minute and they were gone. Just… fucking disappeared. The only one they found alive was a little girl. She said she was blindfolded and that she heard drums and smelled something burning. She ran when she had the chance.

"Everyone who was known to be a cult member got brought in for questioning, but they didn't have any

118

evidence. But that was enough to get the cult to disperse and I guess that was the end of it."

"That's kind of fucked up," Reuben said. "But why are they targeting Lou? He'd have been a teen-ager."

She shuffled through one of the stacks of papers from the library. She squinted at the two she chose, try-ing to make sure they were the right ones through the faults of the photocopier. She handed them to Reuben- a newspaper article that read *Cult Leader Found Not Guilty.* He could barely tell what was going on in the photo- grainy and dark. But there was just enough clar-ity within the darkness of it that he could make out the whites of a woman's eyes. A smile that seemed out of place, but genuine.

"This is Lou's mom," Reuben surmised.

She nodded. "He doesn't like to talk about it. Like you said- he was a teenager."

"That doesn't make any sense," Reuben insist-ed. "It says she wasn't guilty."

"Not only was she not guilty, but several years later they found out that the thing was a hoax." She sifted through another pile, handing him a printout of a sadly short blurb decrying the kidnappings as such. "The cult members were mostly activists and were in an ongoing battle with Syracor, who wanted to buy out some of the land that the cult used for religious rea-sons. When they were like… 'pffft-no,' they staged this kidnapping thing, sent the kids off to another state, and blamed the cult. Everything was staged."

"Well, they looks like they didn't get the land," Reuben surmised, not entirely convinced that she was telling the whole truth. She could have made all this up during one of her all-nighters. "He's still doing his thing out in the woods and he's got that giant garden out across the river."

She sighed at the mention of the garden. Did he detect a hint of jealousy? "They couldn't build anything that close to the river without running into an erosion problem. They found that out halfway through their hoax and decided to go through with it just for the sake of being petty."

Reuben conceded that this was a possibility. "So… if it was a hoax then why are people so paranoid?"

She shook her head, leafing through the articles like there might be an answer there, but she knew there wasn't one. "You know how people respond to fear," she said. "You said it yourself: fear makes a lasting motivator. No one ever sees the follow-up report. Even the people that saw the report didn't want to believe it. They don't like not knowing who to believe."

"And after his mom was outed as one of the leaders, everyone treated her different. People stopped buying from her, they were struggling to get by. If you think that window stuff is bad, this was much worse. She was fighting that kind of stuff daily. It finally slowed down when Lou was old enough to take over, people started throwing the word 'dementia' around and she went down the hill to some assisted living thing. Then Hayden went off to travel the world and the only one left of the Rhodes family was Lou. So it's on him pretty heavy to be 'the normal one' of them."

"That's one hell of a story," Reuben said. And in a rare moment of empathy, he looked at the stack of papers she'd handed him with Lou's mother nothing but a smear of black on cheap newsprint. "I can see why this shit makes him nervous."

120

Jane shifted uncomfortably in her chair. "So. You sounded like you had a plan. Let's hear it."

If this were a different book, this is where they would kiss.

Lou had the distinct idea that Jane and Reuben were trying to get him out of the house. Perhaps it started when their opening statement was as follows:

"Lou, we need you to get out of the house tonight." It came, surprisingly, from Jane's mouth and not Reuben's.

"Why," Lou said, but then he stopped himself. "You're going to do something stupid, aren't you?"

"What? No," Reuben defended. "We just see you've been working hard and probably could use a drink or something."

The suggestion was met with another long pause before he started looking for his messenger bag and the keys attached to it. "I'm not paying your bail," he said before heading out the door. "Call me when you're done."

The door shut gently behind him and Lou's footsteps faded as he left the floor. "You made it sound so hard," Reuben said.

"Normally it is. He doesn't like going where there's lots of people unless he has to. Except if it's with people he likes, which isn't a whole lot. Getting him to leave when I'm having a session is a chore- he usually just blocks it out." She shrugged, then checked her phone. "The camping trip is supposed to start in a couple hours. We need to get going."

Over the past few days, the site had received a handful of comments. As is often the case with crypto-zoology and other subjects of disbelief, they were all crassly worded and highly skeptical. The word 'fake' was thrown around a couple times, mostly in all-caps and with a handful of exclamation marks.

It did not take much time for Jane to figure out the author of the majority of these comments. This was, after all, a town of less than one-thousand people and most of them were out in the hills with no Internet access.

"He's this douchebag hipster that is cynical about soap," she said. Reuben wasn't sure if that was literal or if this was an idiom out here. It could go either way, honestly. "And he talks a big game but you can use his shadow to tell you how many months of winter are left." Okay, there was no way that one could be literal. Rural Pennsylvania had a thing for groundhogs, no matter how far away from Puxatawney you were.

And he could be found, predictably, at the weird little bar that Lou occasionally went to. He could especially be found there if there was something that he was mad about, and if anyone so much as whispered the word 'Krikadoo' in his vicinity he immediately would be inclined to expound upon your infantile gullibility… but with less syllables.

It was so easy to get him to buy you a drink if you had a pair of tits and never wore a bra. All Jane had to do was flutter her eyelashes and show a little side-boob and he was buying drinks for the two of them.

And it only took a couple of drinks for him to feel cocky enough to put his money where his mouth was and agree to spend a night in the woods, within the circle of trees where the Krikadoo was known to visit.

"You know," Reuben presumed, as they began their trek through the trees. "It's okay to admit that you dated him."

"What? Dated Chet?" Her response was a long, sustained farting noise. "Oh man… whatever."

The circle of trees came towards them and they no longer hushed their voices. "I saw Lou stuff his mask and stuff into a tree. I wanna say it was about a mile in."

"He does that so no one can link it to him if they find it," Jane said, lighting a cigarette. "I keep telling him that he needs a better hiding place, but everything out here is dying anyway. People only come out here when they're lost or looking for him."

The smartest decisions, in Reuben's experience, were the kind that left just a tiny window of exploitation. In this case, Lou left a lot of little holes. That, on the other hand, was not very smart. He might not be in this scam for the long haul, but he was going to patch a few of those up before he left.

They reached the circle of stones where Reuben had first seen him put on the mask. Wishing that he had brought gloves, he began digging through a hole in a rotting tree trunk in search of the disguise. He pulled it out, the entire thing covered in dirt and decomposing wood. The fact that Lou didn't seem to care about the number of diseases that he could be exposing himself to by wearing this thing made Reuben uncomfortable. The man was braver than he lead on, but not about the right things. And this thing wasn't just a mask- it was really some animal's skull. He was holding the dirt-covered remains of a wild animal in his hand, and Lou was the kind of guy that casually put this on his face.

Reuben shuddered.

Jane had wadded an old sheet inside the skull mask. The entire thing was hung up on a fishing line over the branch of a pine tree that was looking less than evergreen these days, not weighing too much now that it was just a bunch of muddy fabric and some bone. They weren't about to try to make any kind of harness, Reuben didn't know how and Jane didn't care enough to teach him. Instead, Reuben climbed a tree and lead the dummy up into the air while Jane judged it for cheesiness.

"Do you think it would look more fake if it had sticks for arms," she asked.

"You want him to look like a snowman?"

"Not like... sticking out of his side. I mean under the fabric, so it spreads out."

"This thing is already a bitch to hide and you want to make him bigger?"

She shrugged. "Well, right now he looks like a cheap Halloween decoration."

"Well, is Chet afraid of Halloween decorations?"

She looked off into the distance, taking the question a bit more seriously than he'd put it. Just about when it looked like she was going to come up with and answer, the snap of a twig echoed against the trees, followed by loud voices.

"Shit, that's Chet," she said, scrambling up the tree. Reuben gathered all the material and tried to secure it to a branch where it wouldn't be seen.

"Who is he talking to?" Reuben tried to look through the leaves that he was hiding behind, but they were still too far out for him to be able to tell, and it was getting dark.

Jane climbed higher. "That looks like his friend Drew."

"That means literally nothing to me," Reuben whispered.

"Well, you asked. I don't know what you expected."

"How much more does this complicate our plan?"

She didn't answer. Instead, she climbed higher to get a better view. Reuben was, admittedly, looking up her shorts, wondering if she continued to not wear underwear even when she was wearing denim. It was amazing to him how she could pose there on that branch without moving for such a long period of time. He was starting to get bored of watching them.

They set up camp, posing on the stone pieces presumably as proof that they were there. They weren't paying a whole lot of attention, it looked like.

"I'm gonna be pissed if they came out and only planned to stay an hour," Jane said. "I told that fucker he had to stay all night."

The light was starting to wane as the sun sank behind the hills and the two men below began shifting towards the center. A minimal effort had been put towards gathering wood and mostly they ended up with two armfuls of dry twigs, which they piled into the fire pit.They compensated for their lack of wood with a liberal application of lighter fluid.

It ignited in an impressive 'whoomph,' flames almost reaching Reuben's perch. The two men below responded with a high-five.

And as soon as the fire reached a somewhat safe level, they sat back among their belongings, and opened a few beers. And in just a few moments, the air had a delicate sourness to it.

"Damnit, I knew that jerk was holding out on me," Jane said. "Now I have to scare him."

"On a scale of one to ten, how good is the weed out here?"

"It's the kind of stuff you find in the ditch. I think he buys it from the Amish."

"That was not on a scale of one to ten."

She shrugged. "I dunno… maybe a four?"

He took a whiff. "That smells like a two."

"I'm not playing this game with you. It's not good, but it's what we get around here."

"Hey man, I hear talking," Drew said, standing up. Reuben and Jane immediately stopped talking and hid behind the pine needles of her branch. Flashlights blinded them, casting a shadows like rotten teeth through the branches they hid behind. They hugged the branches, staying very, very still.

Across from the circle, a raccoon lumbered through some struggling bushes, causing the entire bush to shake. Both Drew and Chet spun around to investigate the noise, taking the attention away from them.

Reuben felt a tugging at his leg. "Now!"

"Now?"

"While they're high and their backs are turned."

Reuben untied the rope holding their glorified Halloween decoration to the tree, and the entire thing plummeted to the ground. "Shit," he hissed. "I thought you secured the other side!"

"One of us is gonna have to go down there and get it," she said. "Before they find it just laying there. You're closer."

"Me? You're the one that didn't tie it down!"

"You're closer to the ground! You could survive

that jump, I'd break something."

Reuben was about to call bullshit, but the men were returning to the circle. He jumped down and grabbed the mask, fully intending on returning to the tree and calling the mission a failure.

"Dude, I heard something over there," Drew said.

"Man, you're trippin'," Chet mumbled. "I told you there's nothing out here but fuckin' raccoons and shit."

"This was big, though."

Jane was up in the tree, motioning that he should hide. But the two of them were coming in close and there was no way he could get out of there without being seen.

The show must go on.

He grabbed a dead branch from the ground and stuck the dummy's head onto it, making it taller. He hid beneath the layers of old sheets and heavy canvas and held that branch close to him, trying to make himself smaller and smaller. He darted behind trees and skirted the campsite until the two men had their backs to him again.

And then he waited.

"See, I told you there was nothing-"

The two of them stopped, mid-turn, when they saw the creature standing on the edge of the light. It was easily seven, maybe eight feet tall and seemed to grow out of the darkness. Light shone from the deep, empty sockets of a bare, white skeletal face. They could see nothing more than that skull, hovering heads above them and still as a stone.

"Dude, do you see that?"

"I think that's the Krika-thingy," said Chet.

They didn't move, wondering if their eyes were playing tricks on them. But then the creature lunged forward, shadows overtaking the light of the campfire and those eyes deep in the pits glowing wild and bright.

Chet and Drew jumped back, ready to run but also filled with morbid curiosity. "Maybe it doesn't see us," said Drew. "We can follow it and see where it goes."

"Are you out of your mind?"

The Krikadoo lunged forward again, sweeping into the fire pit. Sparks and embers flew in every direction. Still, it swung and lunged forward, completely unfazed by the flames that clung to it. Worse, even: the fire coiled itself into its shadow and left a trail of char behind. A creature of shadow and embers and burning ash followed them.

"Shit, I'm out of here," Chet said, before running. Drew followed shortly behind, screaming into the night.

As soon as their screams faded, the entire thing collapsed and Reuben emerged from the shadowy sheets, rolling around on the dry leaves to put the fire out. He learned the hard way that whatever canvas material Lou used for this costume was not flame retardant. The hem of his pants were burned for sure, and the sleeves of his shirt were singed. When he finally stood back up, his face was covered in ash.

A slow clap echoed from the branches of the tree in front of him. "Encore," Jane said. "I liked the part where you caught fire."

Reuben had a witty retort, but it was unintelligible between trying to expel smoke from his lungs and also attempting to breathe.

Jane climbed down from the tree, surprisingly

not making a lot of noise in the process. Reuben began gathering up the costume, inspecting the thing for holes made by fire and other things he would probably have to explain to Lou when they got back. Meanwhile, Jane was investigating the stuff that Chet and Drew left behind.

"What the hell are you doing," he asked.

"They left beers out here," she said. "And there's still some weed if you want it."

"I'm not smoking a two."

"Suit yourself, snob."

He let out one final pathetic cough. "I'll take one of those beers, though," he said.

She tossed one over to him and in a miraculous feat of dexterity he actually caught it this time. "You're the epitome of good health, Reuben," she said. "What is this? Day six of your concussion?"

"And yet, you're the one that gave me the beer, doc."

She shrugged, opening her own beer. He watched her chug the beer with an odd fascination until something caught his eye. It moved slowly through the trees, and not in an animal way. It wasn't in an ethereal way, either. But it was steady and it was slow and it was not stopping.

Reuben abandoned Jane to go investigate. If anyone saw them out here, it would blow their cover.

He followed the sound of rustling leaves as something walked with heavy feet through the ground cover, barely bothering to lift them. In the dim light cast from the flickering campfire, he couldn't see much of what it was… but he could see dreadlocks and that was just enough for him.

"Lou, I thought I told you to go out," Reuben

said. But Lou trudged forward, as if he hadn't even heard him say a word. "Lou," he called again, but the man was passing him. Eyes forward, unmoving except for the sluggish shuffling of his feet. "Goddamnit," Reuben said, stumbling to walk backwards and keep up. He snapped his fingers less than an inch in front of Lou's face and there was still no response. He shuffled past, as if he were sleepwalking.

The word 'dementia' echoed horrifyingly in his mind. His only encounters with it had been the pitying whispers about a seldom-mentioned uncle. He only knew that someone had to be with him at all times or he would start wandering and get lost, that it was a shame- such a shame- and that they should have seen the signs earlier but what can you do…

Lou slowly chugged towards the river.

"Shit," Reuben mumbled, trying to decide what to do about this. He was not equipped to handle this kind of thing, but the more he hesitated the faster he was going to head for the river, and the red rock that marked the sandbar where it was safe to cross was a good mile away. He needed to get help or he would just keep going, but Jane was already gone and there was no one else to turn to.

Meanwhile, the idiot was going to drown in that mud water. He matched speed and put his hands on the man's shoulders, trying to shake him awake. "Wake up, man!" But his pace never changed and Reuben found himself pushing against him with all of his weight, feet slipping on the damp soil, then wet soil… then mud.

What was it that Lou had said about the undercurrent?

"Woah, we can't cross here," Reuben said, stepping aside as soon as he felt water seeping into his shoes. But Lou moved on, unwavering. "Lou, we can't- goddamnit..." Forcing himself far out of his own comfort zone, he waded deeper into the water and tried to pull him back to shore but even his arms were tensed and snapped straight back to his side.

The water was up to his shins and Reuben was still trying to push him back, and then up to his knees when Lou stopped. Reuben couldn't even tell that he wasn't still walking: the river made everything seem like it was moving even if it wasn't. He stopped pushing and Lou's eyes seemed to widen slowly, focus, adjust to the darkness.

Reuben let out a sigh of relief when he lifted his head. In the dim light, he could see confusion in his face, but at least he was lucid.

"Christ, you scared the crap out of-"

Who he scared the crap out of became a minor mystery for a moment when Reuben took half a step backwards into the steep dropoff in the middle of the river. He fell into the water and struggled to find purchase in the loose sand and gravel before being swept up in the current. Lou was still slow to move, still unsure why he was standing in the middle of the river, but very sure that regardless of the context, Reuben was not going to be able to survive his trip downstream.

He dove into the water, arms outstretched and letting the current take him, hoping that he could catch up to him in time. He felt every solid object that he passed, until he finally grabbed ahold of something soft and warm. It wasn't moving.

He felt his way up Reuben's body until he found his arms, taking ahold of him by the shoulders and dragging him towards the bank of the river. The current threatened to pull them further down the river, beckoning them both to embrace the release of death, but their combined weight offered enough resistance that eventually they popped up out of the surface.

He was out of breath by the time they reached the bank, Reuben weighed more soaking wet than he thought. They'd traveled almost a half mile down the river, just before the water became rough. The soil became rocky and rough and climbing out of it was a battle, but the shore was waiting for them.

He laid Reuben out on his back along the river bank and hovered over him, trying to catch his breath.

This was the part where he was supposed to perform CPR and save this man's life. He knew that, but it has been well established that Lou didn't know near enough about first aid to use it correctly. Did he do mouth to mouth first or did he do the chest compressions or was there something else he was supposed to do? He didn't know, so he did the first thing that came to mind.

He panicked.

He alternated between almost pressing on his chest and almost giving him mouth to mouth, but each time he tried he stopped because he thought 'what if I'm doing it wrong and I kill him?'

He was about to try it anyway when Reuben's entire body shuddered and he spit about twenty ounces of water from his mouth. Lou backed away, Reuben sat bolt upright and coughed the remaining river water out of his lungs.

"Oh thank god," Lou said. "I thought you were..."

Lou was interrupted by the sound of Reuben promptly throwing up. He sat back down, folding himself at the knees and resting his chin on his arms and waiting for the retching to slow to a stop.

"What the hell were you doing," Reuben croaked through a tight throat.

"Me? What the hell were you doing?"

"I was saving your ass," Reuben insisted. "Your turn."

"I was the one that dragged YOU out of the river, not the other way around."

"You know, when I told you to go out tonight, I didn't think you'd go sleepwalking."

It was clear by the look on his face that Lou wasn't sure how to respond. "I… what?"

"Sleepwalking," Reuben repeated, making gestures as though he were dissecting the word with his hands. "Its when you walk in your sleep."

"I know what it is I just... " Again, Lou didn't know what to say. He buried his head in his hands, trying to remember how he got to the river, but it was a jumble. "I don't remember sleeping. I went to get coffee," he said. "I… I heard a noise and then I was standing in the river."

Reuben's head was still reeling, but even through the dizziness and fog he knew at least one thing: this was bad. A person who blacked out and went wandering could not be trusted in a scam. What if he talked in his sleep, too?

"How's your head," Lou asked.

"My head?" His head wasn't any concern. Lou's head was the one everyone needed to worry about.

Lou tapped his temple. "Your concussion. That can't have helped any."

Reuben ran his fingers against the cut on his head. He'd been so worried about Lou that he'd forgotten to take stock of his own well-being. "I feel like someone stuck me in the spin cycle," Reuben said. He'd hit a couple rocks on the way down- he could tell he was going to have bruises on his arms and on his left knee. Amazingly, his head was still intact, even if it did feel like it was still full of water.

"Yeah," Lou said, but he wasn't responding to anything that Reuben said. He was focusing on the surface of the water, the moonlight glinting off of it. It looked peaceful from here. "I don't know what's wrong," he said finally. "Maybe it's just stress."

"That sounds like a question for Dr. Jane," Reuben said, wobbling to his feet. He could feel his legs again, though they ached, and that was a good thing because he did not want to spend the rest of the night laying on the ground, nor did he want to make Lou carry him.. "Look, let's just get inside. I'm going to need a shower."

A lasting motivator

News that the Krikadoo was real spread fast in a way that only gossip can travel in small towns. Chetnd Drew took it from there, telling everyone who would listen about their encounter with their very own Boogeyman. They became minor celebrities any time they were in public, everyone wanting to know what actually happened.

"It was ten feet tall," Chet would say.

"And it had claws for hands," Drew would add helpfully.

"And howled like a wolf…"

The website got more and more hits, people would send Jane their stories and she would publish them no matter how ridiculous and fabricated they might be, on the basis that if they kept it too factual people would stop believing in it. Reuben didn't understand the logic, but it was keeping people interested and that was all he wanted.

Whenever things needed shaking up, Jane would take one of Chet or Drew's belongings, dip it in mud, and leave it somewhere conspicuous so that they would start talking about how the Krikadoo stole their wallet.

And that was fun, but it wasn't exactly results.

Results happened some days later, when the stories were no longer fresh and became whispers in the background.

Reuben had offered to help out in the flower

shop, if for no other reason than to keep an eye on his investment. After the incident at the river, Lou seemed distracted and Reuben caught him sometimes staring off into empty space. Not that it mattered much when he didn't have customers, but if that was a sign that he was unstable, he was looking for it.

After all, he was officially there for surveillance.

A woman came into the shop, a seven year old boy trailing closely behind her. She looked nervous, Reuben noticed. Lou probably noticed, too- a florist is not someone you generally see in a state of anxiety.

"Stay close to me, Geoffrey," she whispered. Reuben could tell that it was spelled with a 'g.' That's the sort of details he picked up on. Lou looked up from his arrangement, only realizing that she was there because she spoke.

"How can I help you," he asked, a little bewildered that someone would be willing to come in after a solid week of people being scared off by the fact that the place looked like it was falling apart.

She handed him a crumpled list, written in round handwriting. "Day lilies, Oxeye daisies, Crimson clover, Sweet Pea? Is this for… a centerpiece," he asked, unsure what to make of the odd combination of wildflowers. They were not often requested, mostly he only used them as fillers for bigger pieces.

The woman was tight-lipped, holding Geoffrey-with-a-G closer to her. "It doesn't matter. Do you have them?"

He stared at the list. "I do," he said. "One moment." He disappeared into the narrow storage room, leaving Reuben alone with the two of them. He quickly made the connection between the nervous behavior and a list of native flowers. A crooked smile appeared on his face, knowing that this woman was afraid because of something he did.

"Where are you planning on leaving them," Reuben asked.

"Its none of your business," the woman retorted.

"Well, I mean, you can't just leave them any-where and expect him to know they're meant for him." Her eyes went wide, now aware that he knew that they were meant for an offering. "Be a shame if he didn't know."

She pulled her son closer. "Tell me."

"You didn't hear it from me, but there's this circle of stones by the river. You're going to want to leave it there. Once you've put it down, don't look back. Keep your eyes forward and head straight home."

Words tried to form in her mouth, but she seemed caught between accepting the advice out of fear and refusing it out of stubbornness. Before she could decide, Lou emerged from the back with an armful of flowers. She jumped forward, taking them in her free hand, forced a crumpled fifty dollar bill into his hand, and ran out the door.

"Don't you-" Lou began, but the door slammed behind her and he was talking to no one. "-want your change?" He stared down at the bill, still a little bewildered by what had just happened. He turned to Reuben to see if he could explain. Reuben was grinning. "What did you say to her?"

"I gave us a way to quantify our success," he said, looking at the money in his hand. "Twenty-five of that is mine."

Slow to calculate, Lou said: "Sixteen and sixty cents. We're splitting it three ways."

"I remember saying half for me and half for you

two."

Lou sighed and shook his head. "Don't do that to me," he said. "I've got enough trouble without you trying to nickle and dime me. We're splitting it into thirds."

Reuben put his hands up. "Fine, we're splitting it into thirds. But I'm the one risking my ass."

"I just want to fix my goddamn window," Lou mumbled.

"Well, if things keep coming the way they do, that'll happen in no time."

In true small-town fashion, news of where to buy and set offerings spread within the space of a week. Lou had a special bundle of wildflowers, priced higher than he would have normally set them at Reuben's request, which he would sell out of daily. He was making visits to the garden twice a day, once before work and once after, to keep up with demand. Jane was processing submissions to the site constantly, to the point where they were becoming dull.

And Reuben? Reuben was taking pictures. Taking pictures of Lou talking with customers, of people's offerings. The ones of the ritual site and the offerings were sent to Jane for the website. Of course, he posted all of these things anonymously. He liked the look she got from seeing other people participate in their hoax. It was the closest thing to real emotion he ever saw in her.

Of course, rumors did fly that it was Lou all along. It was the logical conclusion, after all. But there had been a handful of people at the cafe that night and they had seen him there- that was enough to keep the police off of his back for a moment.

Though, they did find it rather odd that he had vanished without leaving a tip.

Focusing on work had given him a chance to recover from the worrying bout of somnambulance. It didn't happen again and nothing out of the ordinary was going on. Reuben let him work in peace, figuring that he was doing just fine now and Reuben didn't like being downtown where all the cops liked to hang out.

His scam was doing well and he was raking in a pretty good paycheck from Needles. He just needed to pick a time to send the evidence in and cash in.

In the meantime, he spent a considerable amount of time napping; finally healing the damage that might have been done to his brain.

He awoke from one such nap because he could hear a rhythmic tapping noise. At first, in his half-awake state he thought maybe Jane was having another one of her sessions again. But as he began to roll over to ignore it, it became clear that the tapping noise was happening in the room. In front of him. He opened his eyes and Jane was sitting in front of him.

To his dismay, she was fully clothed, impatiently tapping her foot against a chair leg.

Also to his dismay, she was holding his phone.

"I thought that some of those photos looked purposely blurry," she said. He struggled out of the futon and made a grab for the phone, but she pulled it out of his reach.

"Did you hack my phone," he demanded, scrambling to his feet. The pressure from his knee got stuck between two of the support slats and he faltered.

"Your pin was just a bunch of fours. It was the closest thing you could do to dollar signs." He reached for it and she pulled it back, standing up and getting a reasonable distance from his reach. "Got some interesting photos here," she said.

"Those are personal," he said, trying to get his leg unstuck.

"Personal photos of... us setting up our hoax, it looks like." She made a look of mock surprise. "What's this button here? Looks like the delete button to me."

"Don't you dare."

"Oh," she said, taking the phone into the next room. "I dare."

By the time he freed his leg, she was already out the door. There weren't many places she could run to, he'd catch up with her eventually. When he made it out the door, she was on a bicycle riding circles around the house.

"Give that back," he spat, hoping no one was around to see this display of immaturity.

"I don't think so," she said. "I can't have you walking around with an abundance of blackmail, now can I?"

He quickly gave up on trying to reason with her and attempted to cut her off mid-circle. Of course, she swerved out of the way and changed course entirely, heading towards the line of trees and looking up from the phone only occasionally.

It was about one quarter of a mile down the trail that she started to slow down, putting more focus on the phone than trying to outspeed Reuben, who was surprisingly fast when properly motivated. He easily overtook her and cut her off down the trail, jumping in front of the wheel and taking ahold of the handlebars. He grabbed for the phone, but she jumped off the bike and started running.

"Goddamnit, Jane. Give it back!" Before she could get too far, he reached for her and grabbed her by the arm. In what could only be described as a 'dance move,' she spun him around and twisted his arm behind his back. She took his other arm and all but tied the two of them in knots behind him, pushing him to his knees. One kick to his back and he was face-first in the dirt.

"How long have you been following Lou," she demanded, dangling the phone in front of his face. This close, all he could see was a red and black blur, but he knew that it was a photo from the drum circle, before they'd officially met. He made a sudden struggle for it and she shoved her heel into the space between his shoulder blades.

"This isn't what it looks like," he said, mostly as a placeholder until he could come up with a good expla-nation. He didn't have a convincing lie prepared and he couldn't think of anything.

She deleted the photo and Reuben gritted his teeth. "It looks like you've been stalking him since you got here, so I'm all ears."

What were good reasons to stalk a person other than being paid to do it? Well…

"I just wanted to get close to him, okay," he said, exhaling as if it were hard for him to admit this.

He felt a little bit of the pressure release from his back, but not enough to really let him go. "Are you saying that you had a crush on him?"

Reuben paused, trying to decide if this was the lie he really wanted to tell. "Yes." But she wasn't letting up any of the pressure.

"I don't buy it. You can't expect me to believe that you stalked him and set up this scam just so he would notice you."

"I am not good with my own emotions," he said into a clod of dirt.

"I've noticed," she said. Reuben had been hoping that this would end the conversation, but she didn't let up on his back any. She also wasn't giving him his phone back. Out of the corner of his eye, he could see her really thinking about whether or not she believed him. "On the one hand, I don't know if I believe that you'd go through all of this because you're into him, but on the other hand- this seems like the dumb shit a boy would do. So you have me at kind of an impasse."

"Do you want me to prove it?"

She chuckled, imagining various scenarios of him trying to provide proof of his feelings. "That would be hilarious, but I'm going to make this simple for you." She drove her heel further into his spine and spasms ran up and down his body. She dropped the phone on the ground, the photo deleted. "If you do anything to hurt Lou," she said. "It doesn't matter where you go or how fast you run. I will find you and I will kill you." She gave his back a final kick before stepping off of him and getting back on her bike. "Have ya got that?"

"Why are you so protective of him," he called to her as she sped past. "He can take care his own goddamn self!"

"Because I owe him, moron," she called.

He desperately wanted to get in the last word. He wanted to get up and chase after her on that bike and get her back.

But instead, he just laid there in the damp dirt, trying to decide if he was in too deep yet.

This was not his first death threat. Any time spent handling other people's money was time spent being threatened in one way or another. No one ever meant it.

This was different. That was money. You can

144

always find a way to get that money back if you're desperate enough.

But this was about people. People aren't money. If you mess up a person, they might never be the same again.

But was that too deep?

Not with all those photos deleted it wasn't. He was going to have to start over. He was going to make some cash out of this somehow, and twenty dollars a sale was not going to cut it.

In every lie, there is a kernel of truth just waiting to be slathered in butter and thrown in the microwave.

Reuben's first instinct was to avoid Jane as much as possible, and that was not an easy thing to do in that tiny house. So, as a result, he made a stronger effort to be out, which meant spending more time traveling between the ritual site, Lou's shop, and the garden. There was no possible way to recreate the photos that he'd lost, even though he did consider trying to escalate things for the purpose of getting some footage. But for now he'd have to sneak a few of him here and there.

However, the actual taking of the photos was fewer and further between than he had intended- as much as he didn't want to do any actual work, it was hard to watch Lou digging in the garden and not feel like he ought to be doing something with his hands. It was not a rare sight to see him with a shovel and asking what he could do to help. After all, if he was going to be taking a cut, he might as well get his hands dirty.

Even when he thought that the place should be dry and over-harvested, the garden seemed to produce more and more each time he came to visit- often new and exciting flowers would be in bloom the next morning. That is to say… they would be exciting if Reuben had any interest in horticulture. Which he most certainly did not. He was just here for the pictures.

And to help Lou out, even if he was planning on

handing him over to Needles when it was convenient. The man did drag him out of the nastiest river he'd ever been in.

Well... the only river he'd ever been in.

It sort of felt… good. Well, he was tired and sore by the end of the day but it had a kind of rightness to it.

He made a mental note- rightness was painful.

The sales began rolling in, and whenever Reuben thought that the last resident of the town had bought one, another wave of them would appear- desperate for something that they could not provide themselves.

The week passed and it was time for Lou to take inventory. A tally was made of what was sold because of the scam, numbers were added up and split into thirds. It was hard for Lou to believe that within the course of a single week he had managed to make and amount of money surpassing five zeroes, and yet he only met the action of splitting it three ways with a half-moment of hesitance. A third of it was going to be plenty- he could go back to his simple life, the hard part was going to be over.

"This turned out better than I thought," Reuben said, taking his share. It seemed a little light to him, but he had concluded some time ago that he was in this for the fun of it rather than the money.

"You say that like you had only so much faith in us," Jane said, rolling her eyes. She appeared to have forgotten about the talk they'd had and was at least acting civil. That worked well enough for Reuben- if she was going to be less hostile, that was one less person to hunt him down when he left. Eventually. Of course, he had to leave sometime. Needles would only wait for him for so long.

"I had full confidence in my ability to pull this off," he said. "I wasn't sure if you guys were going to be able to follow through."

"Is that why you set yourself on fire," Jane asked.

"You.... set yourself on fire," Lou asked in turn, looking up from his second count. He seemed more amused than concerned.

"Look, the show had to go on," Reuben explained enigmatically. "We've moved past it." He studiously went back to counting his cash, while also calculating the paycheck he was getting from Needles. The scam was over, for the most part, and now it was time to think about finding a way to cash in. He'd have to fall back on calling the cops on him from time to time to get back what he'd lost, but now that he knew the guy and where he was going to be most times of the day it was going to be easier.

The question was- do you call them in on arbitrary things just to get that photo op, or do you call them on serious offenses such as the unauthorized farming across the river?

Either way, now he had options. It was going to be easy.

"I can replace my window," Lou said quietly. He had a small sort of smile, the kind that didn't look like it belonged on his face. And that as heartbreaking and all, but the real joy Reuben got was from running the bills through his fingers, pressing his thumb against the center and sliding it up and down, enjoying the crispness, the weight, the…

…texture.

The texture was wrong. What was more, it was

wrong in a familiar kind of way.

"Don't suppose those two hunter guys came in and bought any, did they," Reuben asked.

"No," Lou said. "I'd be pretty shocked if they did. Haven't seen them in awhile now that I think about it. Why?"

Reuben thought about telling him that the cash he had in his hands was counterfeit. Convincing counterfeit, but still detectably so to someone who knew what to look for. But in Reuben's ever optimistic mind, this had the color of opportunity. Lou had only a nominal idea of how to spot a counterfeit. He calculated the scenario: if Lou got caught with a handful of them, there was no doubt that he would have to explain to the cops that he was innocent.

And what better a setting to stage a photo than at the police station?

All Reuben would need is a handful of counterfeit bills. And it was such a smart thing of him to always, always, carry some fakes on him. Just for cases like these.

Lou always woke up at 6:45 in the morning to get ready for work. Even with the added workload, Reuben didn't understand the point when he didn't need to open the shop until nine o'clock. Nonetheless, Reuben was motivated enough to finish the job that he was more than prepared to wake up at four in the morning to steal the man's keys, drop the fakes in the register, and be back before anyone was the wiser. By the time Lou was done trying to talk his way around the cops, Reuben would be well on his way out of this town towards a giant wad of cash.

So when his 4-in-the-morning alarm vibrated,

he was all set. He carefully removed himself from the futon, avoiding the gap in the slats and making as little noise as possible. Lou kept his keys attached to his messenger bag by the door. Reuben quietly muffled the sound of the keys jingling against the carabiner with his hand and waited to see if anyone had heard it.

He didn't hear anything, no one stirring, not even snoring.

No sound at all.

That was almost as worrying as the fact that his bedroom door was open an inch.

Against his better judgement, he came closer, making sure that he was okay. Through the dim light streaming in from the distant street lamp, Reuben could only see one thing.

Lou was gone. There was no doubt about it- he was nowhere.

Reuben panicked.

"Jane," he said through her door. He knocked softly, as if attempting to be polite. "Jane, are you up?"

He heard a groggy moaning coming from beyond the door. A couple fumbling footsteps and the door swung open, her bleached hair tumbling into her face. "What," she demanded.

"Lou's gone missing," he said.

She sighed. "He's a grown man and this is his house. He can come and go whenever he wants."

"You're not worried that he might be sleepwalking?"

The smudged eyeliner made her currently squinted eyes look almost nonexistent. "Why would he be sleepwalking?"

"Sleepwalkers don't need a reason to sleepwalk, they just do it."

"Right, but that's not something he does. He's probably just out gardening or something."

Reuben's facial expression became a series of straight, horizontal lines. "At four in the morning?" Jane shrugged and began to close the door, but was interrupted by Reuben's foot stepping between the gap. He tried not to look like he was in pain as the door smacked into his toe. "Look, he had an episode or something the other night when we were in the woods. He headed straight for the river before I woke him up."

"Is that why you took an hour and a half long shower? We have to pay the water bill here, you know."

"Damn it Jane, this is serious."

She chewed on her lip, trying to decipher what she considered to be the most intense emotion she had ever seen in an adult man in her life that were not directly connected with the concept of orgasm and the fact that she was seeing them on Reuben's face in particular was noteworthy. "Oh my god," she said. Reuben stepped backwards. "You legit care, don't you?"

"What?"

"You for real care what happens to him. Oh my god, that's cute as hell. Its frickin' adorable!"

Reuben had forgotten about that lie. "Yes," he said with a dramatic sigh. "I care what happens to him. Are you going to help me find him or what?"

She was so fucking smug about it. "All right," she said. "I'll help you find him. But I'm telling you, Romeo- he's fine."

Lou's car was still in the driveway, which meant that he probably had not gone far. With the exception of the gas station on the corner, nothing was open this late and that left only one logical place he might have gone: the woods.

"We should check the garden first," Reuben suggested.

Jane went quiet at the mention of the garden. "Great. I spent three years with this guy and I finally get to see his garden- and its uninvited and in the dark."

"I'm sure he'll be too humbled that we were worried about him to be angry. What's the big deal, anyway? It's just a big pile of weeds." She sighed, refusing to elaborate any further. That was fine by him, what she had to say wasn't going to change the fact that he was still missing.

He lead her through the dark, using his phone as a flashlight to see where he was supposed to deviate from the path, but after a week of going back and forth it was almost muscle memory by now. But that was in the daytime. In the daytime, he could clearly see where he was going.

By flashlight, every little obstacle seemed bigger: roots were lifted higher, rocks were moved just enough for him to trip over them. It was as though the path was making a conscious effort to keep them from reaching their destination.

"Are you sure you know where you're going," Jane asked.

He grumbled, feeling it better not to answer.

The river seemed even angrier than usual. Reuben was certain that this was where he was supposed to cross- the big red rock was there to mark its place. But even if the water was considerably calmer here than down the hill, the roughness of it gave him pause.

"You're… sure it's okay to cross," Jane asked. "I mean, we tell people to go swimming in the river when we want them to leave town. I'm not going to give you mouth to mouth if you drown."

"Sure I'm sure," he said. He was not about to tell her that he'd already had a similar enough experience and was not intending on recreating it.

He lead the way still, feeling as though the sand and silt was falling away beneath his feet. Why was this so much harder now than when Lou was in front of him?

As they made it to shore, Jane made a sniffing noise behind him. At first he thought that maybe she'd gotten some of the awful water into her nose somehow. "Do you smell smoke," she asked.

Now that she had mentioned it, once the sharp smell of the river receded he could easily smell smoke. It was a wet smell, like mulch- even though it hadn't rained. Reuben took off, not even bothering to see if he was taking the right path and just following the smell because at this point it seemed like it was a better guide than memory. Jane was yards behind, breathing hard and muttering 'jesus christ' under her breath.

When Reuben finally reached the crude archway that served as an entrance, it was nothing but char, embers of the dying fire glittering like amber stars in a hot, black night. Everything beyond that was similarly burnt: black and still smoldering. Reuben fumbled with his phone again to illuminate it.

"Lou," he called to the plumes of smoke. "Lou are you in here?" There was no sound, apart from the nearby river. The light from his phone caught a few rays of smoke, but no movement. "Lou," he called again, trying to see if he was behind any of the smoldering bushes.

The fire had swept the entire garden, and he could tell by the way some pockets were more progressed than others that they had been started strategically. His foot kicked a broken bottle- some home-made molotov cocktails. The entire garden was a little damp, and it was not the result of rain. He could smell the slight metallic notes of the river water saturating the garden, just underneath the smoke.

"I don't think he's here," Jane said, wandering around the smoldering path. "Man, he is going to be pissed when he finds out."

"I think he already knows," Reuben concluded. "Someone doused the place with river water. Otherwise this place would be nothing but ashes." He swung his phone in a circle to get a good look at the whole place. "Are you worried about him yet?"

"Wow. Way to make me out like the uncaring bitch, dude." She gingerly picked up the fried head of a massive sunflower. Her entire body slumped as she sighed. "This is not how I wanted this to happen," she mumbled, cradling the flower like an injured animal. Through the smoke, Reuben could see genuine emotions on her face.

"We can't just sit around and fucking cry about it, Jane," Reuben insisted. "Lou is more important than a bunch of dumb fucking plants."

She kept staring at the blackened sunflower head. "You don't understand at all, do you?" He had to admit, he didn't. "I shouldn't be allowed in here."

"The fuck are you talking about, I'm here all the time."

She paused. "You're…" She halted. "That's different," she started again. "You've been permitted. I shouldn't be able to come here."

"The gate is a fucking bunch of twigs- anyone can just walk in."

She looked up at him. "Well, they can now," she

155

said, indicating the smoke and char. "God… I thought maybe one day I'd be let back in, but not like this. Not because it was dead."

Reuben paused. "What the hell is going on?"

She dropped the sunflower in her lap. "This is a sacred place, Reuben. I can only be here if I'm forgiven or if it dies."

"Forgiven of-" Reuben began, but here she looked so small. Small, helpless, lost. He imagined her as old as seven, covered in dirt, in black and white. "You're the girl," he concluded. "That Juniper girl. The one they found, the one that outed them all."

"God, you're slow," she said. "They stuck me in a burlap sack, dressed up in hoods and cloaks, dropped me off in the middle of the Circle and gave me room to escape. For all I knew, I had been kidnapped and brought in for human sacrifice." Her eyes went dead again and it all finally started making sense. "How do you apologize to a God for something that you didn't even know you were doing?"

"He's not a god, Jane. He's just Lou. You could probably open up with 'I'm sorry' and you'd be fine."

He was met with a long sigh and then silence. And for once he could truly call it a silence- where he could hear nothing but his own breath. The fire had scared everything off- birds, bats, bees. Even the over-fed bullfrog in the reservoir was quiet.

But he didn't like this kind of silence.

"I take it you know who did this," she said, rolling out of the silence like a wave.

"A couple of guys had been bugging him," Reuben said, knowing that it could only be them. They probably didn't care too much or the phony bill he'd handed them, either. With all the time he'd been spending at the shop lately it would have been hard not to realize that they were friends. Damnit, this was his fault. "They thought that Lou would tell the police that they were hunting without licenses-"

"I think you mean permits. They got a cabin or something?"

"On the other side of the hill, I think."

"I say we set it on fire." She began fishing in her pockets for a lighter.

"What!?"

"They burned his stuff, I'mma burn theirs. It's fair."

"No," Reuben protested. "We have to find Lou first. Before we do anything, we find Lou. He could be anywhere."

Jane wrinkled her nose at the idea that Reuben had taken the role of the sensible one. "So where do we start?"

Reuben sat back on a soot-covered rock, buried his head in his hands. "I don't know," he admitted. This was so much worse than he thought it was going to be. Everything was going great and suddenly it was awful again. Story of his life.

"What's that," Jane asked, breaking him out of his spiral. She was pointing to something behind him, and he followed the direction of her finger to a warm light across the river.

"I dunno," he said, craning his neck to see any further detail- but for the most part it was just a dot of light through the trees. He traveled to the edge of the garden to get a better look. "That looks like it's the Circle."

"Do you think that's him?"

"It's as good a place to start as any," he said. He

moved closer, trying to see more than just a bright spot, but there wasn't much to see without getting caught in some of the glare. The light shifted, and in ways that could not happen by a single person alone. "I have a feeling."

"Is it a good one?"

"No."

The way back always seems quicker than the way there, but the truth of the matter is that, when you're worried about something on the other side of a jilted river, every inconvenience- every stone in the wrong place, every root just an inch too high, every wave hitting your feet- makes it seem longer. And each minute spent battling the elements was a minute he could be closer to Lou if it weren't for that fucking crayfish clamping onto his pinky toe.

When the truth of the matter was, the minutes broke down exactly the same way, thirty-four minutes- even with Reuben trying to get there as fast as he safely could, in the dark and much of it barefoot.

The light through the trees was getting brighter now, not only because they were closer but because it was becoming larger. The possibility that Lou was alone vanished completely. The fire, not contained solely by the pit but which had extended into rocks surrounding the secondary circle, was ringed with the silhouettes of at least a dozen people, heads bowed.

"Jane, what does this look like to you," Reuben whispered as they got closer. "Because it looks like a cult to me."

"All the members ran after the controversy, though," she said, motioning for him to keep his distance and approach only slowly. They inched closer, keeping their cover in the shadow of a tree, and trying to find Lou among them. They weren't moving, not even talking to each other and only staring intently at the ground. When he couldn't find his face, Reuben started looking for his body in the silhouettes.

But none of them had his wide shoulders or his long hair. Others were coming at a slow and steady pace, making their way through the trees. He could see them slowly emerge from the darkness, emotionless and unblinking into the light of the fire to join the circle.

Reuben and Jane noticed one thing each.

"None of these people look old enough to be members," he said. These guys couldn't be much older than thirty.

"Why are they all in their pajamas?"

He looked closer. Flannel pants and boxer shorts appeared to be standard attire. White tanks were optional. This seemed somehow more peculiar than if they were all in meeting in the nude. Jane peered through the glare to see if she knew any of them.

"That's Blaine Dobson, he works at the 7/11." Granted, it was hard to see much of them between the darkness and the fire. Everyone looked like they had pits for eyes. "And Angela Kitterow in the pink booty shorts right there. That one is… um… Charlie Bloom…"

"So what do they all have in common? Other than standing half-naked in the woods, I mean."

"Well, they're all in their twenties, but so am I so that's not it." She made a wholly unattractive face while she thought. "Did any of them buy from the shop?"

Reuben went through a mental list of names and faces. "No, I don't think so."

159

She made that unattractive thinking face. "Charlie and Angela are the oldest siblings and Blaine is an only child. They're firstborns!"

"And their parents wouldn't have left an offering," Reuben concluded. "They'd have figured that they were safe because the last time it was just toddlers."

"*The Krikadoo always gets his share,*" Jane recited. "Good thing we didn't use that tagline or the entire town would be scared into believing and we'd be in real trouble."

Oh, right in the guilt. In the minute and a half that they had been trying to figure it out, more and more people began to arrive and join the circle. The approximated dozen doubled to twenty-four with more coming in. Each one of them looked as though they were lost inside a dream.

And none of them were Lou.

Soon it was not limited to twenty-somethings. The age spectrum had widened to thirties and forties, the occasional teenager. The circle had stretched to the outer ring of trees and when that began to be too small another circle formed within, and another… until the flames from the fire nearly licked the unwavering faces of the newest attendees.

As the place filled with people, Jane began trying to count. She was doing math in her head and trying to remember just how many people she knew to have older siblings or none at all. "This is like a quarter of the town," she said. "There's no way this many people would have known about it… unless…" she pivoted to face him. "You did use that ad, didn't you," she accused.

"It was better than the blank space you had."

"Well great job, genius, now we have a prob-

160

lem."

"I didn't see this happening, obviously," Reuben gestured widely to the mass of people.

The influx of people trickled to a stop, easily a hundred people crammed into that little space. Then a hundred fifty, and more still coming in. When it seemed as though the ring of trees could contain no more, the last person joined them and closed a small gap at the center. Five rings of people, amounting to easily two hundred, lifted their heads in unison and turned their attention to the fire burning in the middle.

A strong gust of wind blew in from the east, the flames almost extinguished but for the raw, glowing embers. It was so dark that he could see the reflection of the moon in the whites of their eyes. The fire hissed and cracked as it slowly came back to life, but Reuben couldn't see it.

Standing in the way of the fire was a figure easily eight feet tall, draped in a heavy cloth. He could see no face, only eyes that glowed red and hot and patient.

"I found Lou," Reuben whispered.

Jane appeared over his shoulder. "No way," she said. "That can't be him."

"I can't think of anyone else that fills out that getup the way he does. It's him."

"Okay so now what, genius? Because the first thing I want to do is call the cops."

"And tell them what? That your roommate is heading what looks like it's going to end in human sacrifice?" He recognized some of the faces as being out of uniform. A handful of the police force was already here.

"If it gets someone to intervene, then I don't care. I will call my roommate out on human sacrifice."

Everything was intensely quiet for a moment.

Slowly, Lou lifted his hand and gestured with an open palm towards the river. Every head turned to follow the motion, then their bodies, and they slowly began to walk that way. They progressed a slow march towards the river, their feet barely skimming the tops of the dead leaves.

"They're all going to drown if they keep going like that," Reuben said. The giant shadow that he was pretty sure was Lou stayed behind the crowd, still directing towards the river as the throng of people thinned. "I'm going to talk him down."

"Are you insane?"

"You call the cops or whatever, but I'm not doing anything unless I know what exactly is going on here."

"You're an idiot, but whatever." She backed away, slowly at first but soon began running. The crowd passed by him and it was not long before Reuben was left alone with Lou.

For a moment, Reuben thought that maybe he hadn't been seen and was waiting for Lou to drop the act. But the only motion that he made was to slowly lower his hand, and there was no relaxing of the shoulders, no sigh as he fell out of character. Lou just stood there like a statue while the flames slowly grew back to their height.

But his eyes were straight forward, staring him down like burning suns.

"Okay, Lou," Reuben said tentatively. "It's just us now, you can cut it out." Nothing changed, but for the intensity of the light in his eyes.

Lou didn't seem to be moving anything but his head, following him as he moved closer. With each footstep, he began to doubt that he was talking to Lou.

"If this is all about the fire, Jane's on her way to the police right now. We can get it all sorted out. You don't have to do… whatever this is."

Reuben didn't know a damn thing about what was happening, if he was to be honest with himself. But what he did know was that something was wrong with Lou. And Lou was his friend, even if he was going to rat him out in the morning.

The closer he got, the more nervous he became that Lou wasn't talking. Maybe this was connected to the sleepwalking or the dementia or something else, he didn't know. It was scary, but he was here, ready to take whatever unpredictable thing he had for him.

"Come on, man, just take it off."

From somewhere within him came a small spark of stupidity, which he chose to call 'bravery.' He reached up, grabbed the mask by the holes where its eyes should be, and pulled down.

And there was a brief moment where he half-expected it not to come off.

The person behind the mask was not Lou. No, that's misleading. Lou's face was behind the mask, but it didn't feel like Lou was the one behind those bright, shining eyes.

And Reuben's first thought was an extremely coherent 'that's not right.' But his second thought was that if this wasn't Lou, then there was only one person that it could be.

"Okay," Reuben said to the Krikadoo, backing away slowly. Now that his eyes were focused solely on him, it was clear that he wasn't too happy with him. He thought that maybe Lou's face was hiding a scowl. "You can have your mask back." He set it on the ground and began walking backwards. "No hard feelings, right?"

The Krikadoo knelt down to pick up the mask, Reuben blinked and it was gone, leaving a pile of crumbling dirt behind. Reuben deflated about two inches, deciding not to ask any further questions and that whatever was happening tonight was essentially over and that it was best to leave.

He took another step backwards and felt something dark and hot envelop him. He didn't need to look up to know that the Krikadoo was behind him, but he did anyway and saw the gleaming white bone covering Lou's face.

Reuben jumped and the Krikadoo reached for him, a wide swing of a massive, caped arm. He ducked, pivoting quickly and unsure if he should try to talk to him or just run. He always had been able to talk his way out of trouble, but… Lou was far from hearing him.

This, he decided, would qualify the situation as 'too deep.'

And when things got too deep, the best decision was always to run.

He took off towards the faintly glowing lights of town, feeling as though every root, rock, and branch were being moved specifically to be in his path to keep him behind the line of trees with the glowing eyes of the Krikadoo behind him and gaining with every bounding step. He didn't look back, he never looked back- but he knew that no matter how fast he ran, the Krikadoo was always just an arm's length behind him.

The air became thinner, easier to breathe the further he got from the river. When he stepped over the line of shrubbery that marked the town borders, it was as though he had stepped clear of a thick cloud. He kept running.

Screw all of this, he thought. Every single bit of it-screw it. He dove his hands into his pockets, located his car key, and had it out and ready before he even reached the street he'd parked on. He was going home, he was going to tell Needles he needed to get someone else to do his spying. This was too dangerous and he was a money launderer, this undercover kind of thing was not for him.

Hell, maybe he'd be fine if he just didn't tell Needles anything. Just drop off the face of the earth for awhile and come back, claim he'd lost his memory and point to the scar near his temple. In the meantime, he could take himself as far away as a tank of gas would drive him. Maybe Maryland? They had stuff in Maryland, he'd find something to do before someone found him.

His hands were shaking when he got to his car, making it hard to turn the key. He kept looking behind him, wondering if the Krikadoo was still following him- hoping he wasn't but at the same time… it would at least have given him a chance to say good-bye to Lou. When he saw nothing- no glowing eyes and now sweeping shadows- he sighed.

Whatever, it was going to be over.

He slid into the driver's seat and took a deep breath. He was going to drive out of here calmly. He was going to get on the nearest highway and head east. He was going to make as few stops as possible. He was going to forget everything that happened in this town. He was going to drink a lot of very cheap wine.

That was his plan. It was a simple plan, it was a vague plan, but it got him to a place where there were hopefully no monsters waiting in the woods for him.

Now that he had caught his breath again, steadied his keys and tried to re-orient himself. He heard something moving- not outside, but in the back seat of the car.

No.

Hell no.

He felt his heart pounding in his ears, expecting to turn around and see the two glowing pits glaring straight into him. He grasped his keys, positioning them between his knuckles, ready to fight if necessary. As he began to slowly turn around, whatever was back there shifted. There was a sound like a 'whoosh' and something was put over his head like a canvas sack. He struggled, tried to pull it off of him, but it was being held down.

One heavy blow to the head, and he was out.

There's more than one crook in Harrenville, PA
-----------.

When Reuben woke up, he had a splitting headache. He made a mental note to stop waking up like this. Sound was swimming inside his cranium, bouncing off of its curved walls into an echo chamber. He thought...water.

His neck was killing him. Neck and shoulders. He tried moving his arms but they were stuck behind him. He attempted to lurch his whole body to get himself unstuck from whatever was holding him back, but it just make him hurt more. His head was reeling.

Water, no- it was too regular of a sound. And it didn't smell like he was near the river. That was something that he was bound to notice. Wood? Ink? But when he opened his eyes, he couldn't see anything but the inside of the bag that was over his head.

Why the hell would Lou put a bag over his head?

He heard footsteps, and then the slamming of a door. The churning sound became quieter. Okay, things were starting to make sense: he was in a room, there was something outside, and he was in the company of two people. He was tied to a chair- zip ties, not handcuffs, so they weren't police unless there was some serious budget cuts.

He just about had it figured out when someone tugged on his bag and pulled it off of his head.

The room spun just a little bit as his eyes adjust-

167

ed to the light and his head rolled along his shoulders. The blurry blob on the right side of the table was tall and thin, the other was round and probably angry.

"Needles," Reuben said. His voice croaked when he tried to speak. He cleared his throat and blinked his eyes, trying to get a better understanding of his surroundings. Chair, check. Table, check. Zip-ties, unfortunately, check. The place was made out of wood and Reuben was not used to seeing Needles in a place that had things derived from nature, so it was a little odd to see him backed by a wall made out of logs. The same could be said of Shark, but he made a point of not looking at Shark, to avoid angering him somehow. "Man, I am so glad to see you," he lied.

"It's been weeks, Reuben," he said. It was so odd to hear Needles sound mad. Of course, he never saw the guy actually be happy but the even, business tone that he used with people generally made him seem emotionless. And for the most part, Needles did keep that flat tone. The anger was subtle. "The boss is on his way."

Reuben felt like something was holding onto his lungs. Moretti didn't come down off his throne unless there was a problem and he did not want to be Moretti's problem.

"Okay, I don't have any pictures, but I can explain," Reuben said. "I had like thirty good ones that would have been great, but you know how easy data loss is these days. I can get something on him- I swear it-"

The door opened again and Reuben stiffened, thinking that Moretti was on the other side. There was that churning sound again, something metallic but soft. And… the smell of something chemical. Bleach, maybe?

Needles approached whoever was on the other side and Reuben craned his neck to see who it was, but could only see a little bit of their face through the crack in the door.

Reuben didn't know what Moretti looked like, but he knew it wasn't that. The man was rotund, needed a shave and wore flannel. His hands were stained with ink.

Somewhere in the fog of events that had elapsed in the past week, he recognized that five-o-clock shadow. He craned his neck to see if he could get a better look as the door closed. He sat back in the chair, trying to decide whether the confusion he was experiencing was legitimate or if it was because this had to be his third head injury since he got here.

Needles took note of that confusion, and a pointy little smile started to curl up onto his face. "I think it's time you learned why you're here," Needles said. He set a yellow envelope on the table and pulled out something glossy. Photos. At first he thought maybe they had gotten ahold of the photos that Jane had deleted, but that wasn't right. The angles were wrong and… he was in them. They were all pictures of him and Lou- at the shop when the window broke, outside the bar.

"You've been having someone follow me? Why?"

"Well, we needed proof."

"Proof? Proof of what?!"

"Proof that you were getting a little too close to the cops out where our counterfeiting business was distributing."

Reuben narrowed his eyes and tried to follow

what he way saying, but it was a hard thing to manage. But now that he'd said the word 'counterfeit,' that was definitely the sound of a printer in that other room. Tim's hunting buddy's hands must have been covered with ink, maybe something had jammed. All of that made sense but… "Lou's not a cop," Reuben said. "And if you tell me that Jane's a cop, I am going to laugh."

"Lou's only relative in this town is the Chief of Police."

"Okay, now that's just incorrect. He's not related to anyone here since his brother went to Europe or whatever."

Needles pulled another piece of paper from the folder. In the top right hand corner was a picture of the cop that had been called to the park, the one that talked to Lou like he knew him. There was a big, bold text at the top that said 'Chief of Police- Mike Vollinger' right there at the top. "This is Lou's uncle."

"There is no way that they're related," Reuben insisted. "They don't even have the same last name."

"Hate to be the bearer of bad news, but surnames are not what makes people family."

"They don't even look alike!"

"Also not what makes a person family."

It was starting to dawn on Reuben, in a slow but stubborn way, that Needles wasn't joking. And he started putting puzzle pieces together, and the gears started clicking, and the moment he realized that there was a reason he was zip tied to the chair was the moment that all of his breath felt like steam. "You sent me here," he said. "You set me up."

Needles gave Shark a friendly look. "See, I told you he'd figure it out eventually." Shark didn't do anything, feeling mostly bored.

"Why," Reuben asked. "After all I do for you, and you do this shit to me?"

Needles seemed exhausted by the question. "The thing is, Reuben, you don't actually do anything for us."

"Bullshit, I do plenty!"

"And actually, you're a strain on our resources and a huge security risk. The only reason we hire you is if we can't get ahold of someone better and-" He made a gesture like weighing scales with his hands. "Turns out there are plenty better people out there."

"I am not a security risk. I am locked up tight like a safe."

"I gave you a week to do this job. This job right here, which was so fucking simple that my nan could have done it, rest her soul. But here it is, week and a half later and... what are you even doing? You're fucking around doing some stupid side project, and this ain't the first time I've had to clean up after you. Soon as you get paid, you go straight to the bar and what do you do?"

"Uh, drink? That's what you do at bars, man."

"I have to send someone to keep an eye on you because you'll do stupid shit like drop hints. Do you have any idea how many cops visit that bar?"

Reuben had to admit, but only to himself, that he did not know how many cops came and went from the bar across from his store. He always thought he could spot an undercover cop from the way they walked, but... he was starting to think that he was wrong. Which was ridiculous.

"And then there's the goofy shit, which you pick up any time you get ten feet away from your block." Needles curled his hand into a goose egg. "You have

171

zero foresight. Like that scam you tried to run with the Girl Scouts."

"Eight dollars for a box of Thin Mints is price gouging and I'm just saying they can do better. And you could have just told me not to instead of pulling this elaborate bullshit."

Needles rubbed the bridge of his nose between his two long fingers. "We did. Several times."

"Okay, so you could have just bought my silence. Everyone would be happy."

"Paying you off," Needles laughed. "Would imply that you mean anything to us. But you don't. And if it were up to me, I'd just put you alone in a room with Shark and call it a day. However, people have been looking into some of our 'missing persons' and the boss has decided it's best to address things like this personally. So he's on his way up here to take matters into his own hands."

Reuben was suddenly aware that his fate did not look good. All the blood drained from his face and the throbbing in his head seemed stronger. There was a good chance that he was going to die. "I'll tell him that you set me up."

Needles laughed. "Yeah, he's heard that one before." There was another knock on the door, and Needles rolled his tiny eyes in its direction before standing. He opened the door with just enough room for Tim to fit his head in the crack. "What now?"

Tim was awfully quiet for someone who had a gun, but then again he had already demonstrated that he didn't know how to shoot it. His voice wasn't much more than a low rumble.

"What do you mean it's jammed," Needles spat. "What am I even paying you for?" Another low rumble.

"You... don't know what's jamming it? It's simple, Tim- paper goes in, cash comes out. The only thing that could be jammed is paper. Just reach in and grab it!" Rumble rumble. "It's... moving?" He sucked on one of his pointy teeth, then whipped his head around to address the Shark. "Sounds like they're going to need your tiny hands, Shark." He crooked his finger towards him and Shark stood, keeping an eye on Reuben. "Don't worry about him," Needles said. "He's not going anywhere."

This left Reuben alone in the room, with a crack in the door so they could hear anything that happened while they were in the next room.

One thing that Reuben like to think set him apart from your average Joe was that he knew just what to do in the event that he was being held hostage. He knew the very minute that Needles came knocking on his door that there would come a day when he would be tied to a chair, he just didn't think that his kidnappers would be someone that he trusted. But none of that mattered to him now- Needles was dead to him and he had his escape all planned out.

Though...

Whenever he played this fantasy out in his head, he was tied down with fiber ropes instead of plastic zip ties. His kidnappers would be arrogant enough to put him in a room with something sharp enough to cut through them and they weren't... quite this tight. The decor was... considerably less rustic.

Reuben was beginning to think that Needles had a mild point when he had said that he has zero foresight. He was beginning to think that a number of his problems were avoidable and self-inflicted.

But that was quitter talk, and his mother- although prone to leaving her car in neutral and naming her only child after a sandwich- did not raise a quitter.

This was not an interrogation room in the back of a butcher shop. It was not meant to hold anyone hostage. There probably wasn't a basement, otherwise they would have put him in there. But he was above ground- there was a window to his right. If he could get out of this chair, he could open the window, take out the screen, and escape.

Ha, and Needles said he didn't think things through.

But of course, there was the matter of the chair and his current position of being stuck to it.

Through the crack in the door, he could hear a discussion going on. Needles' reedy voice rose above the others. "What the hell is that thing?"

"Ben thinks it's a snake, won't touch the thing," Tim mumbled.

"Shark ain't afraid of snakes," Needles offered.

Even with the churning sound of the printer, he could hear them talking. Whatever he was planning on doing was going to have to be quiet. He took a deep breath and sank back into the metal folding chair. Without being able to see his hands, he could tell that the left zip tie was slightly looser than the other one. It was not loose enough that he could easily slip out, but if he was going to get out somehow, that was the place to start. He needed a free hand. If he rotated his wrist just a little… he'd heard you could do that to get out of a zip tie if you were willing to work at it.

He leaned forward, trying to straighten his arm as much as possible with everything aching. The edge of the zip tie was cutting into his hand, but he could feel it bending under the pressure and pulling at the fleshy parts of his thumb. He was so close up until the part where his knuckle got in the way, but he kept pulling.

He heard the 'pop' before he felt the pain, and when he felt it he clamped down on his lower lip to keep from screaming.

What they don't tell you is that if it's too tight, you're likely to dislocate your thumb. The pain froze him up completely, his entire body shuddering from it. But damnit, at least his hand was free- he had a fighting chance at getting out of here.

That is... if he could get his hand to stop shaking.

He took a glance at the window, thinking that maybe it was closer than he thought it had been, but alas- it was not. He thought he saw something moving in the vague moonlight and he suddenly felt cold. Lou was out there still. He didn't know if what he saw moving out there was him, or if he was still the Krikadoo or if he was still mad, but... he was still out there.

Even when he got himself loose from the chair and escaped the cabin, he would have to get to a car fast and drive as far away as possible- and Needles was not the type to leave his keys in the ignition.

So which was it going to be? Wait around for the angry mob boss or get out and have to deal with an angry demi-god?

It was a tough call to make, and with only one useless hand free- it seemed that the choice was going to be made for him in the long run.

Yelling was happening outside of his room. "Shit, what the hell is that!?"

"Kill it!" There was a scuffle while two people went after whatever it was and the other two went to the opposite side of the room. Two gunshots, then silence.

"It's still moving, it's still moving!"

It was at this point that Needles came back into the room, followed by the two hunters and an ink-covered Shark. They all looked scared.

"So are we gonna negotiate the terms of my release or what," Reuben said, hiding his free hand behind his chair.

"Shut the fuck up, Weller," Needles snapped. "There is something very weird going on and I don't need you yammering."

"Weird? What weird?"

"I said shut your hole!"

"I spent the last week learning about the weird shit in this town because you set me up with a cult figure and now you don't want my input. Anything that happens is going to be on you." Through gaps in the woodwork, Reuben could hear shuffling outside. A lot of shuffling- more than a hundred sets of feet. All the firstborns had been heading here, not the river. It was anyone's guess what they were going to do, but he had a feeling that very soon they were going to be in a lot of trouble. "Sounds to me like the whole town is here. Can't imagine they'd be too happy about what you did to one of their sacred places."

Needles turned to Tim. "What the hell is he talking about?"

"Your buddies here thought that a garden around the corner was just a touch too close to this operation, so they set it on fire," Reuben explained. "I'm guessing that doesn't sit right with some of the locals."

"What's that thing out there?" Tim pointed to the door.

"How the fuck should I know? I've been in here the whole time."

"It was like... some kind of plant thing," Tim said, making a waving motion with his hand. Reuben recalled them yelling about snakes. "It was moving, like it was crawling around."

"Purple and pink flowers?"

"Yeah."

"You have to let me out of this chair."

All eyes on Needles. "No," he said.

He sat back in the chair, feigning disinterest. "Fine. You've pissed off a demi-god and his worshipers, this place is going to be covered with those things in five minutes, and I'm the only one who knows how to stop it. But sure- we can just sit tight."

"I'm not falling for it," Needles said. "I may not know what's going on here, but I know you're full of shit. If I cut you loose, you're going to run and leave us here."

Damn, he'd seen through his plan. Well, to be fair, it wasn't a very solid plan. Suddenly, Tim's eyes went wide and he began shaking his leg. They all backed away, except for Tim who was busy yelling 'get it off me, get it off me.'

Reuben looked under the table to get a better view of what was happening. From beneath the crack in the door, a vine had twisted its way around Tim's leg and was quickly crawling up towards his knee. He kicked wildly, trying to get it off. He gave it one big kick, breaking the vine loose from the door and flinging it into the air. Everyone jumped- especially Reuben, who got a face full of vegetation before it bounced off of him and landed back onto the table.

It writhed, separated from its mother vine but still alive. Reuben braced for it to jump straight for him, but instead if began coiling back towards the rest of

177

them. Shark grabbed it and held it taut to keep it from moving, but the vine simply grew; extending beyond its severed edges.

Tim pulled out a knife, ready to attack it if it came near him again, but in a moment of impulse joined Reuben on the other side of the table.

"What the hell are you doing, Tim," Needles asked.

"They're not going after him," Tim said. "What if he's telling the truth?"

"Yeah," Reuben added. "You didn't consider that, did you?"

"We got this under control," Needles assured, just as Shark gave a sudden jerk to keep the now five-foot long vine in his grip. "The man's a liar. Not even a good one!"

Tim struggled to make his decision, but only a moment of temporary loss of control was enough to persuade him to start cutting the ties at Reuben's feet.

"Ben, restrain your friend," Needles ordered.

Ben also hesitated. "But… he's got a point."

By the time they'd decided that this was how it was going to be, Tim had cut his right hand loose. As he was preparing to cut what he thought was the the last tie, Reuben reached around and grabbed the knife, jumping out of the chair. He stood in the corner, poised and ready to attack. Shark's hands were literally tied up and getting tighter by the second.

"Ha," he laughed.

Ch-chk. "Drop the knife, Weller." The knife immediately fell out of his hand onto the wooden floor and his hands went over his head.

He'd forgotten about guns. Reuben had figured that since he had Shark at his side all the time that he had no use for one. But it had already been explored that Reuben is not the greatest judge of people.

"Looks like I'm outvoted by you superstitious morons," Needles continued. "But I am not just going to let you walk out. Now, we are gonna get out of here, and you're going to show us what you can do- if that's anything. And maybe we can renegotiate your usefulness with the boss when this is all over. But if I even think you're gonna run, this bullet goes right between your eyes. Got that?"

Reuben wanted to say something snide, but that was not going to happen when there was a gun involved. He nodded. Needles motioned with the gun that Ben should open the door, and lead Reuben out by gunpoint.

The cabin was not big to begin with, consisting of a large living room and then bedrooms, bathrooms, and kitchens appearing to be tacked on as an afterthought. It might have actually been a hunting lodge at some point; the decor reflecting that with a poorly taxidermied deer head hanging over the door.

The printer took up a corner nearest the door, and seemed in fact to be several printers hooked together. A pile of blanks sat in a box on a chair, waiting to be made into currency. They hadn't been particularly great about keeping their workspace clean, and evidence of daily drinking was tallied in the form of beer cans on every surface.

But none of that really seemed to matter because all of it was covered in living, moving vines. They were crawling in through the gaps in the woodwork, coming up under the floorboards, wrapping around every conceivable object within their reach. A spectrum lamp next to the printer, Reuben's guess was that it was to check bills in a better light, was a popular place for them to gather. A cluster of deep purple and delicate pink flowers were blooming under the light, pulsing slightly as though they might be breathing.

There was not a place that he could step without coming into contact with one of them, and every one of them seemed to be connected in one way or another. Touching one meant touching the others and he was afraid of that. He didn't know if they were ignoring him for a reason or if it was just a fluke that it hadn't reacted to him in the room. He didn't even know what he was supposed to be doing in the event that they somehow were being friendly with him. Was he just supposed to ask them to leave them alone so they could get out? The fuck kind of surreal bullshit was that about?

Needles was still behind him with the gun pointed right at his head, a constant reminder that no matter what happened here- there was a good chance that he was going to end up floating face- down the river by sun-up.

They weren't actively attacking him, but they were crawling towards the door behind him at a rate that was making the rest of them uneasy. A quick glance back at Shark showed him that he was starting to have trouble taking control over the one in his hands- trying to tie it up into itself, but it would just form new shoot and start finding new things to cling to.

"Back up," Reuben said. The four people behind him seemed perplexed. "Back up! Are you going to trust me or what?"

Needles begrudgingly motioned for them to step back. Reuben took a deep breath, preparing himself to do something either brave or stupid or both.

Before anyone could question what he was

doing, he grabbed the chair housing the box of blanks, pulled it towards him, shut the door behind him and blocked the door with it. He pulled out all the printer equipment from the wall and created a barricade of electronics and a book case full of counterfeits before running straight for the door.

Well, tripping straight for the door. There wasn't a single bare area on the floor where he could step without stomping on something squishy and alive. They were ignoring him so far and he wasn't about to call attention to himself by tromping on them if he could help it. The vines were heading steadily towards his captors, crawling over his pile of stuff and under the cracks in the door.

They were starting to break the floorboards, even- tearing new holes that they could come through. It seemed unending, forever creating more offshoots and roots. The shouts from behind that door became more frantic and not directed solely at him. The gun fired once, twice, followed by more yelling.

They became thicker, faster, more aggressive. The entire wall became covered in seconds. Any sound coming from that room was muffled and incomprehensible, but Reuben imagined that the reason there wasn't a third gunshot had to do with the gun being forcibly taken from Needles' hand and swallowed into the mass of vegetation.

Well, that was enough thinking for today, and the way was clear which meant that it was time to get out.

Get out. Find a car. Get the hell away from this town. Maryland. They had stuff in Maryland.

Needles' car was just outside, Tim's truck just beside it. He tried to remember how to hotwire a car, but that was not something he'd ever thought he would have to do and not with a hand swelling up to the size of a grapefruit. Needles wouldn't leave his keys in the car, but Tim might. They all left their front doors wide open around here and neither of them seemed too bright even for counterfeiters. But in the second that it took for him to decide, he heard the crunch and rustle of leaves. It began small, as if one person were walking towards him in the darkness, but soon the noise became numerous- a steady susurration that gave him the sensation of being surrounded.

Out of the trees and into the light, the glare of a hundred pairs of glassy eyes reflected back at him, more on their way as they emerged from the darkness. They marched towards the cabin, penning him in. If he wanted to get out, he would have to shove his way through the throngs of people and they were getting tighter and tighter the more he waited. There wasn't even a gap for him to get through with them standing shoulder to shoulder.

And when they finally stopped marching, some still with wet feet from the trek and all of them still staring with their eyes forward, there was nowhere he could go. Reuben heard a thudding sound above him and watched their eyes lift in unison.

He looked up. Standing on the roof was the Krikadoo... yes- there was no doubt in him that Lou was gone and all that was left was this inhuman shadow. He loomed over all of them, unmoving and staring at them with those pinpoint eyes. Reuben felt himself freezing again, waiting for him to come down for him and this time he couldn't run.

The vines began to snake their way up the side of the building, enclosing the entire cabin in living vegetation. He could hear the cracks and pops of wood splintering under the pressure, but his eyes were fixed on the threat standing on the roof.

He heard police sirens off in the distance, but didn't register that they were heading in his direction until he saw the red and blue lights bouncing off the wooden walls. He looked back and there was a line of cop cars coming up the hill- their lights painting the early dawn with violet before the sun even began to stir the horizon. The crowd of people began to loosen, turning their attention towards the flashing lights and blinking for the first time since dusk.

As the disoriented crowd became aware that something was wrong, Reuben turned back to the roof, hoping that Lou would have woken up from his night-mare self.

But Lou was gone, dirt falling from the roof where he'd stood.

He heard the car doors slam and static on their radios. A murmur passed over the crowd as they all began to awaken, the police trying to figure out what to do. A few of them panicked immediately- most notably a woman in her twenties began screaming uncontrol-lably. Reuben slipped around to the back of the cabin while the police's heads were turned.

He made one step around the corner before he heard a crashing noise come from the rear. He tucked himself into the alcove that the back door lived in and watched Needles' head pop out of the back window, soon followed by a rail-thin arm to propel him forward.

"Let go of my legs," he demanded someone behind him; probably Shark.

He had two options: either have to explain to the police why he was the only person here that wasn't drooling or risk being seen by Needles. And since he couldn't exactly explain anything that had happened in the past four hours, he wasn't exactly sure which one was easier.

Or…

...because he was always looking for the 'or' in a situation…

The police had made their way to the cabin and were trying usher the disoriented masses towards the road. Many of them easily complied, not sure what they were doing there in the first place. The ones that were not complying were not doing so because they were in varying states of distress. One officer had his back to him, preparing to make a statement with the megaphone.

Before he could pull the trigger and announce the police presence to whole damn hill, Reuben tapped him on the shoulder. When he turned around, he recognized him as Mike Vollinger. Well, too late to turn back now.

"Pardon me, officer," Reuben said. "I think you should take a look inside the cabin."

The officer narrowed his eyes at him, skeptical. "You're that little weirdo that's been hanging out with Lou," he said.

"Wow. Yeah. Little Weirdo- that's me alright," Reuben said, trying hard to hide the sarcasm in his voice. "But listen, there's a couple guys in there that-"

"You've been putting ideas in that boy's head, I don't want to hear any of it."

He gave Reuben a shove and held the trigger down for a second. Before that megaphone could make it to his mouth, Reuben took one of the raised bills from his wallet and shoved it in Officer Mike's face.

184

Frustrated with the gesture, the officer lowered the megaphone. "Are you bribing me?"

"Just look at it for a second!"

He peered at the bill, first with just his eyes but eventually lowering his megaphone again to hold it in his hands. "This is counterfeit," he concluded, rubbing it between his fingers. "Where the hell did you get this?"

"Well, that place is kind of stacked with printers," Reuben said, pointing to the cabin. "And if you walk around to the back in the next few minutes you might catch a couple counterfeiters trying to escape out the back window."

Reuben could tell that it had already been a long morning for the police force by the way the officer hesitated. But he couldn't help but feel a sense of grim satisfaction when he pressed the lever down on his radio and called for a few others to investigate the cabin.

Well, he had to stick around for that, of course. Mike went around the back, two others entered through the front door. Needles was still struggling to squeeze himself out of the window that Reuben was now very glad he decided against escaping through. The second that he started hearing footsteps coming his way, he began trying to back his way out of the window. He managed to get his head halfway back in by the time the officer arrived.

"Sir," said the officer. Needles lifted his head, which meant the top back portion of his head slammed itself against the window frame. "We're here to search the premises. Do you mind telling me what exactly you're doing?"

Needles saw the badge first, then the rest seemed to click into place. "You got a warrant?"

"I believe we have probable cause," the officer said.

"Sticking a head out a window ain't probable cause."

"I'd say not, but you've got about one eighth of the town on your front lawn and I've got a few phony bills that look like they came from here, so I'd like you to put your hands up for my friends when they get to you."

There was a rumbling sound on the other side of the wall as the officers inside pushed the last of his barricade to the side and opened the door. Needles' head disappeared from sight.

It was about this time that Reuben had decided he was done here and began to walk away. Now that he'd gotten the cops involved it was time to get out, anyway. But before he could even take two steps away from the cabin, a heavy hand weighed down on his shoulder.

"Don't think I'm just going to ignore the fact that you're in the first place, pal," Mike said. An almost unintelligible crackle on the radio mentioned a dollar amount and the printers. "We've been trying to find out where these have been coming from for weeks now. You just happen to breeze into town and bring us right to them while the weird shit starts happening again and I'm not about to just let you go."

"Officer, let me tell you- I had no idea about this counterfeiting thing until about an hour ago."

"I'm having trouble believing you there, son."

"That's a real shame because this is probably the one time I'm actually being honest."

"Needless to say: we're going to have to take you to the station with these guys." He jerked Reuben's shoulder around and put the cuffs on his wrists. Reuben froze at the idea of sharing a cell with them, even being in the same room was not going to end well for him.

"Okay, listen," Reuben said, wincing as the cuffs grazed his swollen left hand. "You could lock me up and that would be the end of it. Or, you could listen to me and catch a bigger fish coming this way."

"Bigger fish, huh," the cop said, skeptically.

"You heard of Moretti?"

"Moretti, you say," Officer Mike said, not letting up any pressure on his cuffs. "I can't tell if you're threatening me or what- but either way, I'm not impressed."

Reuben winced, the dull pain in his hand sharpening itself any time the cuffs hit the fat part of his thumb. What he was about to do was stupid, but it was also one stupid decision in a long line of stupid decisions and at this point he was wondering if stupids were like lefts- they eventually turn themselves into a right.

"Listen: I can give you names."

"Names, huh," the officer said. Again, he didn't seem impressed by that, either. "Don't think your boss is going to like that very much."

"I know. I will be that person, just don't put me in the same room as those guys. They'll kill me first and you'll miss out on an informant. And do I have to remind you that I'm the only person who knows what even happened tonight?"

Silence came from behind him as the cop looked out at the throng of dazed people, slowly thinning out as cars came to drive them home. If anyone recalled anything, no one was talking. "Said he was coming right here, did ya?" He paused. "Tell ya what- I'll count to ten and if you're out of my sight by the time I'm done, I didn't see you. But I've got two conditions."

"You name it."

"You stay in town. If I find out you're gone, I will track you down and I will personally put you in the same prison as those guys. You do have a handful of loitering tickets, if I remember right."

"Solid. And?"

"You find Lou. I know he's caught up in this mess somehow and he won't listen to family- but he likes you for some reason. You find him, you let me know he's alright."

It was hard to argue when the terms of his release included something that he wanted to do anyway. "You have my word."

Reuben heard the scribbling of a pen on paper, tearing on perforation. A slip of paper was pressed into his palm and the cop walked away. Reuben turned around, waiting for something to happen, maybe a nod or- "Are you going to uncuff me?"

"One," the cop began counting.

Cuffs be damned, he broke into a run and disappeared behind the trees.

A hero and a protagonist
are only sometimes the same thing.

There was only one place that Lou would be- he wasn't a difficult man to figure out. Reuben meandered a little bit just in case someone might be following him, then went straight for the thin path leading to the garden. By the time he saw the charred archway, the sun had started to peek over the hill.

Handcuffs were decidedly easier to get out of than zip ties- offering himself just a little bit more range of motion to slip his hand through. He left it dangling from his swollen hand, deciding that it was better not to try that trick more than once in the course of a day.

Lou was exactly where he expected him to be, and that was sitting on one of the boulders next to the now empty reservoir. The mask was off, the tarp was draped next to him, and the wildness was gone from him. Reuben wasn't sure if he should approach or if he should just send a text to his uncle to let him know that he was okay and get a safe distance.

But he was so tired. He felt like he'd been running for too long and as far as possible death scenarios go, this one was at least more interesting than murder by goon with no neck.

This was better.

Lou lifted his head, whether it was because Reuben made a small noise or if he simply sensed that he was standing there, it was hard to tell.

"I'm surprised you're here," he said. "I figured you'd be gone by now."

"The cops want me to stay in town, so I guess I'll be here for awhile," Reuben said, taking a seat on a neighboring boulder.

"Not like you to listen to what the police say," Lou said wearily.

"I'm a complex man."

They sat in silence for awhile, watching the sun fight its way through the trees. Birds awoke and groggily began singing their morning songs. They seemed mostly unaffected by the noise of the previous night, but that was what birds did, he supposed- they put up with a lot of racket and then forgot about it in the morning.

Birds were dumb and uncomplicated, Reuben had had enough of not-talking.

"Okay, so are you going to explain to me what happened or...?"

"I did tell you that I was a part-time god," Lou said. "People didn't talk about him for so long that I forgot what all of that feels like."

"That... actually raises more questions than anything, Lou. You want to maybe... elaborate?"

His shoulders sagged a little bit. "I mean it's kind of hard to explain, really. We had a cult, then we didn't."

Reuben fumed inwardly, unsure if he was being enigmatic on purpose or if this was just what part-time deities did. "That doesn't explain anything at all. People aren't just... part-time gods. We don't do that."

"Maybe you don't. I guess it doesn't make sense to people who live in the city."

"It doesn't make sense to people anywhere."

Lou sighed. "I guess not." He glanced at the mask and the pile of rags. "It's not easy to explain, Reuben. I just grew up knowing that the Krikadoo was real and that one day he would choose me and we would just have to share a body sometimes. When the cult dispersed, I started thinking it was just a fairytale. But any time someone would mention the name like it wasn't just some joke, I'd get a stirring in my bones. I guess I just wanted to know if it was real or not. Turns out, it is."

"I still don't get it," Reuben said. "I don't get how or why or…"

"There's nothing to get. It just is." Lou was getting a little frustrated at his inability to articulate the most complicated part of his life.

"What does it feel like," Reuben asked, avoiding his eyes. "When you're…" He made a useless rolling gesture with his unswollen hand.

"I don't really feel much," Lou admitted. "I mean, it's scary the first time, but then I'm just… watching. I feel protected, more than anything."

"So… you're aware that you chased me for like two miles last night, right?"

Lou laughed. "Heh, yeah. He… he doesn't like you very much. He thinks you're…"

"Rude?"

"Yeah, I'd say he thinks you're rude."

Reuben considered that for a minute. "He kind of has a point. I've been lying to you from the start."

"I know," he said. "You're a really bad liar. I was willing to believe you for awhile, but there's only so many lies a person can take before it's kind of obvious."

"And you just… let me go on like that?"

"It was entertaining. And… I really wanted to get my window fixed."

Reuben felt an unfamiliar feeling in the back of his throat and somewhere in his shoulders that made them feel heavy. "I came here with the sole purpose of ruining your life. You were just going to be easy money for me."

"Apology accepted." Reuben didn't seem to know that he was apologising, but something about being forgiven made him feel weird. It was a good kind of weird, a light kind of good. "So you're not supposed to leave town," Lou continued. "Are you going to keep to that or are you here to say good bye?"

Reuben dropped his shoulders again. "Well, I can't go home, not after I ratted out my boss. But Lou, I don't know- it's really weird here. People are all in each other's business, you don't lock your doors, you've got local deities, and there's potted pansies every twenty feet on the sidewalk."

"Those are petunias."

Reuben grumbled something about flowers beginning with the letter 'p,' but digressed. "My point is, I don't think I can stay long here. There isn't a place for me in a town like this."

They were silent for a few more moments until Lou spoke again. "There's a little shop on the corner that's been sitting vacant for about three years. I bet it would make a good book shop."

"People out here read?"

Lou shrugged. "I'll be honest: you'll probably end up with a lot of romance novels." Reuben shuddered at the thought. "But if you get too many, you can always give them to me. Paper makes a good mulch."

Reuben gave that a moment's thought. "I guess that's an option."

"But you'd have to give them to Jane first- to make sure that they are truly awful. She can read them aloud to the Internet."

Reuben had a sudden realization. "Why the hell didn't I think about that? I could have made a mint!"

"I think it only works if the person reading is a conventionally attractive woman," Lou explained.

Reuben grumbled something inaudible before conceding. He supposed Lou had a point, but would have been willing to argue his side of it if he had anything available to give a dramatic reading of. But regardless, some money-making endeavors are better left for other people. Lou had stopped smiling, gone back to looking at the ash and soot covered ground with a heavy sigh.

"I'm sorry about the garden," Reuben said.

Lou held a pause, trying to find words but not being very successful. "It's not your fault," he finally said.

Reuben sat uncomfortably with the idea that he wasn't to blame for some of this. "I dunno… if things hadn't gotten out of hand, maybe-"

Lou held up a hand to silence him. "Don't make me angry at you for something you didn't do, Reuben." Reuben jumped back a little at the rare occurrence of Lou raising his voice, wondering if he was going to put the mask back on and grow a couple feet. But he just dropped his hand, dropped his head, and stared back at the damage. "It'll grow back," he said quietly. "That's what it does. People come along, they fuck it up for a minute, and then it grows back. And… I guess that's what I'm here for: I'm here to do the work."

193

"It'll probably be easier if you have two people working," Reuben suggested. Lou smiled.

68567352R00108

Made in the USA
Charleston, SC
15 March 2017